The Immigrant Child

The troubled journey to a new life

ARLENE COLEMAN

authorHOUSE®

AuthorHouse™
1663 Liberty Drive
Bloomington, IN 47403
www.authorhouse.com
Phone: 1-800-839-8640

Published by AuthorHouse 4/4/2012

ISBN: 978-1-4685-4529-6 (sc)
ISBN: 978-1-4685-4530-2 (e)

Library of Congress Control Number: 2012901183

Table of Contents

Foreword

This is a fictional story and any names or resemblance to real life people isn't intentional, and though it is a historical fiction not all happenings in this book actually occurred.

I want to thank all of my friends and family that helped encourage me. If it wasn't for them I wouldn't have been able to finish this book. My classmates and teachers also all helped to inspire me and I want to remember them for everything they helped me accomplish with this book. My Mom and Uncle especially helped me with the final steps in the publishing process and I can't forget that it's their help that has made it possible.

Starting with a bang

"We're pleased to announce that we'll be landing in Toronto in about ten minutes!" the captain's voice blared over the intercom. I sighed heavily and shifted in my seat, a single tear glimmered on my cheek for a moment. I angrily wiped it away. "You're such a girl!" I whispered to myself.

But honestly I didn't know what to think, there isn't a manual on how to feel when your life has been ripped to shreds. I'd been forced from my home, threatened at gun point and now my family and I were about to land in Canada, a freezing cold country that was thousands of miles from my home, thousands of miles from Zimbabwe, Africa.

Why! Why, why, why? I thought angrily, *Why me? Why my family?* But inside I knew the reason. I knew it was because of the war vets, and no not the hero kind you're thinking of, not the kind that make it back from war and everyone celebrates. They were called war vets but in reality they were the worst kind of villain. They said it was because of the natives that had 'been there first' and they were just 'reclaiming' the land - really, they just threatened people, forcing them to give it up. My mind flashed back to that awful day when everything changed…..for the worse!

Three men stomped in, a gust of hot wind flew in with them, and the scent of musty air reached my nose. My heart stuttered as

1

I looked them over. The one in the front held a huge double barrel shotgun the other a machete, the handle of a pistol was buried deep in the third ones hand looking like it had been moulded there. Katelyn shuffled over behind my Mom, peering around her skirt cautiously. Luke patted her shoulder protectively, his handsome features creased with worry. I glanced up at the men again, they wore old ragged clothes, torn t - shirts, and dusty ripped shorts.

"We want to see Mr.Mafeotzy." the one in the fronts gravelly voice drawled. "We saw his truck outside." He said it as an explanation, but we heard the threat in his voice, they weren't here to have a friendly chat with Dad, they were here on very lethal business.

He's not here!" Mom stated bluntly.

"Huh!" grunted 'bossy', his eyes darting around the room suspiciously.

The beeping of the seatbelt sign turning on woke me out of my reverie. Glancing over I saw my four year old sister asleep in her seat and saw my Mom's tears. I felt fury emanating from myself in dangerous waves, Mom must have felt it too.

"Don't be angry Thomas, things happen for a reason! There's more to look forwards to in Canada than to look back to in Africa." She said, as the plane shook from turbulence.

"Thomas!" Mom repeated softly.

I knew there was wisdom in her words; it didn't mean I wanted to hear it. I shook my head making my crop of black hair bounce. I was beyond angry, I was murderous, infuriated, enraged, fuming, and hopping mad all at once; I felt like I was going to scream from all the anger my body contained, like a bubble about to burst. My blue eyes shone with anger and I shook, feeling like I couldn't take anymore. It wasn't fair! Dad and the rest of our family had never done anything wrong, the war vets had only come after us because we were white, just because they could. They only wanted our land; they didn't care what happened to us and would have disposed of us easily, just to gain control of our house and property. These thoughts just made me even angrier. Just when I felt like I was going to burst from the pressure building up inside of me I felt a hand shaking me gently. I immediately jerked up in my seat, just to find a lady offering to take our eating trays and gently shaking me. I smiled weakly at her and passed her my tray. As the plane coasted down the runway I organized my things so we would be ready to leave.

As we walked through the airport I felt utterly alone. My friends and my family were still in Africa, I knew that I was lucky to be here, but I couldn't help wishing things would go back to normal, wishing that things had never gone bad in Zimbabwe. When we finally made it through the long line-ups and stops at immigration and customs I was ready to drop. I passed Katelyn to Luke for a while; I could barely keep myself upright let alone someone else.

"The map back there said that the exit should be straight ahead. Gary and Lucy should be waiting for us there." Dad stated.

We were some of the last ones through, so it wasn't hard for our two parties to find each other. I spotted the two people that could only be Gary and Lucy; they confirmed my thoughts by peering around, then walking towards us purposefully. They had never seen us, and we had never seen them, but somehow, both groups knew they were what the other was looking for. We had never met Gary and Lucy personally, we'd only had a few phone calls and yet they were the whole reason we were here. All I knew about them was that they had to be some of the kindest people on this earth. They had given Dad a job having never met any of us and had offered to take us into their home for as long as we needed to. My thoughts were interrupted again by a voice.

"Josh, Lannette, this must be Luke, Thomas, oh and darling little Katelyn too! Oh my, we're so glad you're here safely!" The woman said in a string of words.

"Lucy, they will be exhausted…" the man that must have been Gary said.

"Well we can take you to the hotel where we will spend the night." Lucy interrupted quickly. A small smile appeared on my face, they were so nice, and there was something about them that was just so comforting.

"Thank you so much!" Dad exclaimed, letting them take a few of our bags. After thirty-six hours on a plane with his distraught family he was looking fatigued.

"It's our pleasure, we're just glad to have you with us." Gary replied as he helped us through the doors and out into the frigid air. "Here are some good thick winter coats," he continued "I know that you won't be used to the cold, but you'll get used to it soon enough."

We all laughed a hollow disbelieving sound that echoed around the roofed parking spaces eerily.

Gary and Lucy had rented two cars, as Dad had an international driver's license so he could drive; Gary and Lucy's rented car was full by the time we had loaded in all of our luggage, so my family and I all squeezed into the second car. No one thought too much about Dad being tired and how that might affect his driving before we pulled out into the highway. The problem arrived when Dad turned out onto a street that didn't have the big concrete barrier dividing the lanes. Dad was tired and not thinking straight I suppose, or at least that's what I used to explain what happened next. No cars were coming so Dad swerved into the left hand lane, none of us thought anything of it because that's the side of the road we were used to being on, we all forgot that we were in the wrong lane, before a humongous truck bore down on us! I blinked and glanced out the windshield again, but the truck was still coming. Dad must have realized something was wrong when Luke, Mom, and I started hollering at the same time. He swerved, narrowly avoiding the oncoming vehicle and our certain demise. As Dad yanked the car into the right lane he was as pale as a sheet.

"I'm so, so sorry!" he gasped "I'm so sorry! Not thinking straight, still in shock, tired, so sorry!" he mumbled over and over.

Mom rubbed his shoulder sympathetically "its okay, it's alright you just forgot, its okay!" She was shaking like a leaf in a storm about to break off. I realized I was shaking too. When we arrived at the hotel Gary and Lucy rushed over to see if we were alright.

"Oh are you okay?" Lucy fussed.

"I'm fine, don't worry, it was all my fault!" Dad muttered, obviously shaken.

New starts and new struggles

I woke up in a cold sweat. *It's just a dream, it's just a dream.* I repeated over and over in my head. *It's just a dream.* I rolled over and rubbed my eyes; in a jolt reality hit me. I remembered the reason we were in Canada now, I remembered the terror of the near accident, I remembered the pangs of loneliness, I remembered the cold, and I remembered the inner pain. No it wasn't just a dream; it was a memory that had played over in my mind while I slept. For a minute I struggled to keep my emotions under control. *Come on, don't be a wimp, just suck it up! Just suck it up!* I told myself over and over; eventually I got my feelings back under lock and key. It was a method that I had learned through recent experiences to help me act normally, to not show any feelings that might betray the turmoil going on inside of me. I know that psychologists say not to keep your feelings bottled up, but that was the only way that I knew how to keep going. Because if the things I kept inside of me started to bubble out, I wouldn't be able to stop until I had let them all out, and in the process of easing my burden, I would load the burden onto my parents, and they had enough burdens of their own.

Luke was already up with my Dad, their heads bowed over cups of coffee. With their identical short black hair sitting side by side it would have been hard to tell them apart except for their faces. My brother had inherited my mother's short rounded nose, while my Dad had a longer, more pointed, slightly crooked nose. My brother had the same chocolate brown eyes as my Dad and same oval shaped face, but the rest of Luke's face had my Mom in it, rounded chin, high cheek bones, and a perfect forehead. All together my brother had a striking, attractive look about him. Often I envied him, with his good looks, athletic ability; and he was funny, as well as smart! It felt like he was always winning some prize!

My Dad glanced up and looked at me with concern, "Are you okay? You were yelling in your sleep, I woke you up four times last night because you were fighting in your sleep. We've decided not to leave until tomorrow. Your Mom has taken Katelyn and gone with Lucy to the pool and hot tub area. I thought I might go and join them, the idea of something warm around here is appealing!" He said, trying to lighten the moment. I tried to smile, but it came out as more of a grimace.

"Well then don't head outside!" Luke said, almost resentfully. Dad glanced at him then looked at me all serious now.

"Don't forget how lucky you are to be here! Okay? I know this is tough on you boys!" he said casting a sidelong glance at Luke again, and I wondered what they had been talking about before I had woken up. "But, no cold weather, or anything else, changes how fortunate we are to be here."

"I know Dad."

"That's my boy! Now I'm going to change and head for the pool area! Who's with me?"

"Me!" I said, trying to sound enthusiastic.

"Are you coming Luke?" Dad asked, more softly now.

"In a bit." Luke replied without raising his head. I glanced questioningly at him before heading to the bathroom to get changed. Gary emerged from his room right behind us and together we descended to the main floor, where the pool was. I walked in and put my towel on a seat.

"Cannon ball!" I yelled as I launched myself into the pool. I let myself sink to the bottom, and opened my eyes. The whole pool looked faintly blue, from the tint in my goggles. I resurfaced and started into a rhythm.

Pull, pull, kick, kick, breath, pull, pull, kick, kick, breathe…

I reached the edge of the pool, and turned onto my back to start a back stroke. By the time I had finished fifteen laps of the small pool I was feeling pleasantly tired, and relaxed.

"You're good!" Gary exclaimed.

"Oh, not really." I replied, embarrassed.

"There's a swim team in Russell, if you're interested." Lucy offered.

"That would be great, wouldn't it Thomas? Mom said cheerfully, though it seemed a little forced. "He was on a swim team in Zimbabwe, well before…"

Silence.

Luke walked in and hesitated before reaching the pool, sensing the mood.

"Maybe we should get out now and head for breakfast before they close up." Dad cut in, breaking up the pool party.

The next morning we woke up early and packed our suitcases into the cars, paid the bill, and left before the city had even started to come alive. We decided that Gary would go in one of the cars with the guys, and Lucy would drive the other with Mom, and Katelyn. As we left Toronto the sun had just started to change the sky from pitch black to an inky blue. I yawned and laid my head against the window, in the distance a plane roared overhead. I clenched my jaw as a wave of anger, and sadness engulfed me. When Luke looked at me I saw that his eyes had lost their twinkle. Now they portrayed how he seemed to be feeling on the outside - forlorn and miserable. He had gone awfully quiet since we had boarded the first plane. My thoughts flickered to last night when Mom had taken me aside in the little bedroom and talked to me.

"Now as I'm sure you've noticed, Luke is having a hard time with the move." Mom had said. "He's talked to Dad and I, and we're trying to help him through it, but if you ever need anything, remember we're here for you and we love you, no matter what you're feeling. It's emotionally stressful when you have to leave all that is familiar and dear to you, it's difficult for all of us to leave our family behind, and trying to embrace a different culture. Everything seems hard right now. Don't forget that it will get better; this move is to provide us with a better, safer future, for you kids as well as for us."

By now Mom had tears in her eyes and they looked as if they were about to spill over. My own tears were on the brink of starting a waterfall down my cheeks. *Stop being a sissy*, I yelled at myself in my head, *guys don't cry, you're not a silly girl are you?* I continued to fight myself until all the tears were gone. I shook my head. *Luke would call me a baby if he knew how emotional I was feeling.* I thought, upset with myself for being so weak.

I don't remember much after that, because I slept most of the way, catching up on the sleep I'd been missing lately. I finally woke up, just before we pulled off at the next town to grab a bite to eat.

"Where are we?" I muttered, still drowsy.

"I'm not sure." Dad replied "but I do know that you just slept for four hours! I'm jealous, I'm so tired!"

"Oh, well why don't you sleep?" I asked.

"I can't get to sleep; my system's still confused with the

different time zones. Well we'd better get out; we have to catch up with the others."

"Hmmm, yeah"

"Well then?"

"Coming" I replied clambering out of the car. As soon as my feet touched the pavement I made a break for the door of the Smitty's restaurant.

"It's freezing!" I complained.

"It is pretty cold for this early in the season, even for us Canadians." Gary smiled.

"In Zimbabwe, the season has come early this year too," Luke commented "only difference is that it's going into summer there."

Anyone looking at our conversations over the past two days would think that awkward silences were the height of fashion.

"Let's find a booth!" Lucy suggested, saving us all from another lapse in conversation.

Dad lagged wearily behind us with Luke.

"Luke, please try to be aware of what you are saying!" Dad said sounding exasperated.

"I didn't mean to make everyone feel uncomfortable," Luke said, his face as red as a tomato. "It just kind of slipped out that way. It wasn't intentional."

"Okay, sorry I over-reacted. I just really want to make a good impression. I start training, or as you could say, working next week Monday, and as they say - first impressions can be lasting. What I'm trying to say is, I'm really nervous and I also thought that maybe you were just being difficult, I'm sorry."

"Me too." Luke added quietly.

I looked away quickly when Luke looked over at me, but he had caught me staring.

"Sorry," he said with a small smile.

"Its fine," I said, "really, it's fine. I know that you're having a hard time lately."

"It can't be just me; you haven't been yourself since we left home either."

"Really?" I hadn't noticed I'd let my guard slip so much. I knew that I wasn't feeling normal inside, but I needed to work on my 'wall' so that it wasn't as obvious to others. From my perspective what was the use in exposing my emotions, like a billboard to everyone? They couldn't change or lighten the circumstances, and besides, it was too hard to explain everything I was feeling. I didn't need people trying to figure out what was going on in my head and telling me how to feel.

"Really, but it seems you're handling it a lot better than I am!"

"Well, things aren't always what they seem." I shot back sharply.

"I didn't mean it like that!" Luke said quickly, "but remember, being a guy doesn't mean it isn't normal to feel sad sometimes, or to show it."

"My names Andy and I'll be your server today. Could I get you something to drink while you decide?" Andy asked, interrupting my sharp retort to Luke.

We gave him our order and he hurried off.

A dream, a tour, and an outburst

We pulled into Lucy and Gary's yard shortly before midnight and by one thirty it started to snow. I pressed my nose against the window pane and watched the snowflakes fall to the ground and melt.

"Can't sleep?" Mom asked softly.

"Mom!" I exclaimed surprised by her sudden presence

"Shush! You'll wake the others!"

"Sorry," I whispered softly.

"Isn't it beautiful?" Mom murmured quietly.

"Until you go outside." I muttered

"What do you mean?"

"Well the snow is beautiful, but the cold that comes with the snow won't be as great!"

Mom chuckled silently beside me. "Well depends on how you look at it. The cold could be refreshing after the heat we're used to."

"Yeah sure, but I'm not used to the cold, and I never asked for a refresher, I liked everything the way it was!" I said, trying not to snap at Mom. I took a deep breath to calm myself.

"Well, I didn't say that it would be easy to look at it that way, but I'm pretty sure it's possible. Let's go back to bed; we'll need the energy tomorrow."

"Right, night Mom!"

"Good night Thomas, I love you!"

"*I think he is here somewhere, and you're hiding him.*" The second one spat at us.

"*Search the place!*" 'Bossy' yelled. "*And if you find him, bring him here!*" *he continued slowly, leering at Mom. Mom looked worriedly at Luke, Katelyn and I.*

"*We told you he's not here; we have his truck for the day!*"

"*Fortunately for you, the others don't see him either!*" *'Bossy' said after the other two men had come back and shaken their heads in disgust. "*But you had better watch out!*" His last threat hung in the air as he raised his gun, as if to punctuate his words with actions.*

I woke up yelling blue murder.

"Thomas, Thomas! Are you okay?" Dad asked, rushing into the room.

"Y-Yeah, s-s-sorry." I replied, hating the way my voice shook. I took a deep breath, "Just a dream, sorry."

"It's not a problem; we were just worried about you. What have you been dreaming about the past few nights?" Mom asked.

"Oh, well, uh…"

"Were you dreaming about Africa?" Dad inquired quietly.

"Yeah, I guess, sort of." I said, still trying to get a grip on the cold dagger of fear that pierced me right through to my heart.

"Oh Thomas!" Mom exclaimed.

"It's nothing it'll pass." I said, rolling my eyes for added effect.

"Thomas, you're probably right, but maybe you should talk to someone! Your Mom is also having bad dreams."

"No thank you! I don't need therapy! Some person I don't

even know peering in at my life, trying to figure me all out, I can deal with it myself!"

"If that's the way you feel, we're not going to force you to see a psychologist, even if we feel it might help you - it has to be your decision." Mom conceded, "We were just going to wake you for breakfast, so wash your face and come on up."

"Yes Mom." I grumbled, still a bit riled from my speech.

"Oh and after breakfast we're going over to the flax plant to take a look around and see where your Dad and I will be working."

"Sure, sounds fun" I replied as I swung my feet out from under the warm covers.

"Good morning, how are you today?" Lucy asked as I walked into the kitchen.

"Good" I said, still yawning.

"Gary just has to check up at the office, then we can go and show you around if you would like and then you can play in the snow. We have some extra snowsuits around here somewhere.

"Thanks, that would be cool!" I said with feeling.

We had a delicious breakfast of eggs, bacon, and toast. When we were done we helped clear the dishes. Gary said he needed to go and check up at the office, so we decided to all go and look around. The office was just a short way away but I had been right when I had predicted that cold weather would come with the snow fall, so we went in Gary and Lucy's Cadillac.

"Where can you drop off the rental cars?" Mom asked on our way over to the office.

"We hired someone to drive them back for us. They'll be here to pick them up tomorrow."

"Well that's nice - now you don't have to drive them back to Toronto yourself." Dad added.

"Well, here we are." Gary announced as we pulled into the parking lot. "Welcome to Pascal's milling"

We all got out and walked to the entrance, unsure of what to expect. We walked in, and a warm flow of air wafted over us. I looked around, my eyes wide. *Wow!* The receptionist's desk stretched across the middle of the large room. Overhead of the desk you could see the hall of the second level. On either side of the desk were hallways that led further back into the big office. On the other side of the passages were single offices. The receptionist desk was raised on a platform and just behind it a room that housed a photocopier, office supplies - such as tape, pens and highlighters - as well as filing cabinets. On the right of us was a pot plant and just beyond that another small office. On our left there was another pot plant, and then a large round table with chairs. Gary led us down the hall on the left of the desk, past the circular table. The photocopier room had three entrances. One from the front desk. One from the other hallway and one on the side we were walking down. Gary showed us his, and Lucy's offices. They were next door to each other. Further down there was an office that was empty except for one desk, a chair, and a coat hook.

"This will be your office," Lucy said gesturing to the office on our left. "Lannette your office will be upstairs."

"Oh, thanks." Dad replied looking in at his would-be office.

Directly to the right of Dad's office was a staircase, leading to what I imagined would be the second floor.

"I've got to go and check up on how everything is going, Lucy can finish showing you around and then we can go." Gary suggested

"Sure." Dad replied.

Just as Gary left a young women of about twenty-five sidled up.

"Is this the new man that's going to be working here?" she asked scooting closer to Dad.

"Yes, my husband and I will be working here. He starts on Monday and I start two weeks after that." Mom answered shortly, pointedly clinging to Dad, her arm around his waist.

"Oh." The women replied absentmindedly, shooting a nasty look at Mom. Dad took a half a step closer to Mom, looking uncomfortable. I glared at this woman that had just suddenly appeared and was making a move on my Dad as well as making my Mom edgy. *Yeesh! She's obnoxious!* I thought to myself. Lucy picked up on the electricity in the air and intervened.

"You should get back to work so we can continue our tour." The woman turned and glared at Mom once more before stalking off wiggling her hips so much they almost touched both sides of the wide hallway.

"I'm sorry about that, Gary will speak to her. We wouldn't want you to feel uncomfortable here." Lucy said as soon as 'miss wiggly hips' was out of sight.

That would be much appreciated!" Dad replied a look of relief crossing his face. He wrapped his arms around Mom.

"Let's continue on upstairs shall we?" suggested Lucy, anxious to continue the trip around the plant. Upstairs there was a long office filled with shelves that had files, and books on them. At the end of the room were a clear space, and a desk with a computer and a few supplies.

"This will be your office when you start work," explained Lucy. Directly across from Moms office was another smaller office with one desk and a white board on one of the walls. At the far side of the room was a door. Along the back was a long counter and above that a window from which you could see the manufacturing part of the plant - there was a plain cement floor and forklifts went around lifting heavy crates.

Way in the back you could just see a long conveyer belt and people milling around it. I took one last look as we left the room to continue on our tour. Back at the end of the carpeted hall just before you turned to go back down the staircase was another door that we had skipped when we had come up the stairs. We entered and found a huge room that had a long window also overlooking the plant. There was a metal stairway that led from a door at the back of the room down to the plant.

"This is the lunch room." Lucy said as I looked around. On the wall going from the doorway were two vending machines and from there three tables that filled most of the room. To the left, just before the large window was a row of lockers.

"Cool!" I said grinning at Luke. He looked at me with a mischievous glint in his eyes and I knew he was thinking exactly what I was - we could have a lot of fun around this place.

Lucy left to go and check in with Gary quickly before we left and welcomed us to look around the office some more. Miss 'wiggly hips' sidled up she glared at Mom with open hostility. Mom wrapped her arms around Dad defensively. I'd had it with this woman trying to make a move on Dad and treating my Mom like dirt. The pressure built up and the match was struck, I was about to blow a fuse. At least I could rant about something now and let off some steam.

"Listen lady, my Mom and Dad love each other very much and are happily married so butt out! Stop glaring at my Mom like that! You'd never have a chance with my Dad even if he wasn't married! You aren't his type so get over yourself! Leave us alone! My Dad isn't interested, so step away from him! Why do you have to be so catty! Stop throwing yourself at my Dad, people that do that are so pathetic! Why can't you just accept that he doesn't like you, so for the last time, leave us alone, and stop throwing yourself at my Dad! My parents have just moved countries, are trying to settle in and have enough traumas in their lives right now! So mmmmph…." I ranted on until Mom put her hand over my mouth, even then I kept yelling at the lady. Mom didn't say sorry or contradict me she just stared at the woman.

"Well, uh," Dad said trying to break the silence, "We should probably go and find Gary and Lucy." He excused us and led us back down the stairway and down to the hall.

"Thomas!" Dad exclaimed "you can't just rave at people; I know that you have had it hard lately, but you can't go around yelling at people! Lannette?"

Mom didn't reply, she just stared at the floor.

"Well then." Dad said, effectively ending the conversation.

We went right and down the hall to another door. We hadn't had a chance to look in here yet. Lucy strolled up to us with Gary.

"Oh, I forgot to show you the lab! You can go on in and I'll show you around before we go." Lucy said.

"Thank you for everything again." Dad said as we entered.

"No problem, we are so glad to have you with us!" Gary replied.

The lab was amazing! It had shelves of things in the middle of the room. At the end of the room was a long table with all sorts of fancy research, experiment, testing tools, and charts on it. There was another door that led to the back of the plant. Gary walked over to a small fridge next to the door. He reached inside took out something. He pulled back his hand that held a can of 'Pepsi'. We walked around and looked for a while, the lab was one of the coolest places I had ever been. When we finished looking around we clambered back into the car for the short ride home.

Gentle Giants

Shortly after we got back James arrived. James was the youngest of Gary and Lucy's children, and I liked him right away. He had inherited his Dads humour and his Mom's good heart. This combination made him a wonderful person to be around. In Africa Thanksgiving isn't celebrated, so Lucy and Gary decided to introduce us to the Canadian custom. Thanksgiving was actually the day before but we had been traveling, so we celebrated Thanksgiving the day after instead. Mom helped Lucy prepare a magnificent turkey that was moist, with rich, creamy gravy. Beside the turkey in the roasting pan they roasted potatoes to go along with the meal. For dessert Lucy whipped up a pudding, ice cream, and a pie she had made just before they had picked us up. The meal was great, and fit for a king. In Africa the cook would have made sadza - a type of corn mixture - and boerewors - a type of sausage - and to top it off we would have had some kariri, a jumble of shredded tomato and onion, with sugar.

After lunch we went downstairs and slipped into the hot tub. The pool outside was drained and had a cover over it to protect it from the snow. Gary told us how some of the kids in Canada liked to roll in the snow and then jump back in the hot tub. I decided to try it with Luke and James. We clambered out of the hot tub and ran out the door into the freezing layer of snow. It burned your skin, and felt kind of gravelly when it rubbed on your arms. I shot up off the ground as soon as I was covered in snow and charged back inside. Luke and James were right behind me. We hopped in the hot tub but then hopped back out again because the water burned us worse than the snow.

"Do you want to go again in a minute?" James asked us when we had gotten our breath back,

"Are you kidding? That was awful! The snow is freezing when it rubs on your skin and then the water burns you in the hot tub!"

"Is that a no?" James asked, laughing

"Well, maybe you could convince me to do it one more time! I'll go with you, as soon as I can feel my legs again!" I replied laughing too.

We ended the day with another great meal of leftovers from lunch. Dad, James, Gary and I finished off a whole tub of half a gallon Rolo ice cream. Later that night laying down in bed the activities of the day caught up with me. Fatigue overcame me but there was one more thing I had to do. I walked upstairs and slipped into the kitchen, the light gleamed off the table. Mom and Dad sat facing each other, I walked up to them.

"I'm sorry, I shouldn't have yelled at her today." I started. Mom looked up.

"It isn't a problem honey, you've been under a lot of stress, but in the future you can't get away with that behaviour, okay."

"I know, and I am sorry, I don't want to make things harder for you at work. Now she'll be mad at me and you."

"She shouldn't have been doing that, but as your mother said you must control yourself in the future, being under stress doesn't excuse your behaviour."

"Yes Dad, I understand. Good night Mom and Dad, sweet dreams."

"Night sweetie!"

That night when I passed into the unconscious world of dreams I dreamed of one of my last memories from Africa.

I stared out onto the savannah, watching the elephant herd. They had a new baby with them. It couldn't be more than a few hours old, and was still learning to use its trunk. It sucked up a trunk full of water, and then tried to spray the water on its back as it had seen its mother, and many aunts doing. It was a hot day with the sun glaring down on us, and a scorching wind blew, offering no cool relief. The elephant baby, its trunk flailing around, was effectively dousing the older elephants. The older elephants didn't seem to mind though. When the baby elephant's water supply had run out it bent down its head to suck up some more from the water hole. He seemed to think better of it and then lay down, wallowing in the mud instead. We all laughed and looked at each other. Katelyn giggled her sweet two year old chuckle, and Luke his throaty guffaw. Dad and Mom stared at us lovingly, while laughing softly too. My favourite part of the little show it was putting on was the time when it stepped on his trunk. It started squealing at the top of its lungs. Even though it was just a baby it's lungs must have been pretty big because even from the distance we were at, the squealing rang in my ears for several minutes after it had stopped squealing. It's mother watched it struggle to get its trunk free from its own foot, but after a minute or so, she realized it wasn't going to solve the dilemma itself. She sauntered over to her baby, her huge strides covering the ground quickly. She arrived at its side and nudged it gently until it lifted its foot.

Elephants are one of my favourite animals. They are so gentle and the actions of the mother had proved again that they are also intelligent. We went for dinner and I almost forgot why we were here. When I lay down in bed that night, I got down on my knees and thanked the Heavenly Father for the laughter *and the great day - there wouldn't be many more of them. Then it hit me in full force why we were here, why we were touring our favourite parks in the area - we wouldn't be here much longer.*

We were doing a last tour of our favourite game parks, and holiday get - a - way's to have some last memories of our old life, of where we came from and so we could remember what our life was before it was ripped apart. We would be leaving the country as soon as the immigration papers arrived, confirming that we could move to Canada. An ache filled my chest and I started gasping quick breaths. The thoughts of leaving my home, and my life here was choking me, I wasn't sure how I would be able to stand it. I felt like I was going to crack into a million pieces. Dad said we would be safe in Canada that we wouldn't have to be afraid. I thought of our twelve foot fence with barbed wire across the top, and our guard dogs. I thought of the gun underneath Dad's bed, the bars over the windows. We had grown up here, so that was just the usual for us - this was our life and this was our home. But then I thought of all the times when I had been afraid, and wondered how things could be so different in Canada. It didn't sound like a different country, it sounded like a different world. The thoughts of leaving my friends and family here shadowed anticipation at being safe, at not having to worry about the war vets.

My dream ended and I sat upright. It hadn't been a screaming, scary kind of nightmare, but for me it was a nightmare none the less. I remembered those last few weeks as I dozed off again into a fitful slumber. My next dream was scary. The 'war vets' stalked through my dreams once more. They couldn't reach me here in Canada physically, but they tormented me mentally.

I woke up at the echoing sound of a gunshot that was only in my head, yelling things in Shona. I stopped quickly, not wanting to wake the others. I looked at my watch. It was about fifteen minutes before six. I knew that Gary would be getting up soon, so I crept up the stairs.

Gary was starting the coffee machine up when I got upstairs. He asked me if I had slept well. I told him I had slept fine, but I didn't tell him about my nightmares. He looked closely at me.

"Are you sure? You've got circles under your eyes and you still look pretty tired. Why don't you go back to bed for a while?"

I shrugged "I feel tired but I can't get to sleep." What I didn't tell him was that I didn't want to sleep - I was afraid the nightmares would come back.

Gary nodded. "The move must be dreadfully unsettling. The different time zone must be confusing your body too."

I nodded in agreement. "It is a bit disorientating."

Gary and I chatted until James walked into the room, still half asleep. We exchanged the normal pleasantries until Gary said it was time for James and him to go. I asked if I could go over with them. As the harvest was in they weren't farming now, so they would be at the office all day and it was close enough to walk back if I wanted; besides we would be coming back for lunch.

"Sure, that would be great." Gary replied.

The shot from my dream still rang in my ears as I clambered into the truck. I remembered the wave of shock and fear that had rolled over me when I woke up. My dream has seemed so real, it had been so vivid, that I found it hard to believe that it was all a dream. I had actually believed that I had been with Dad instead of Mom the day we had been held up by the war vets. I had believed that Dad had been killed. Once I had truly woken up I had realized that it was just a dream, which was when I had stopped yelling. I thought once again about what Dad had said about therapy and I became even more determined to get over my homesickness and fear. I would, I could get over it by myself!

A dream, a day, an apology

We walked through the doors into the office and Gary led the way to the lab. He sauntered up to the mini fridge and yanked open the door.

"Anyone else for a Pepsi?" He asked over his shoulder.

"No thanks." I replied politely.

James was home schooled because he helped with the workings of the farm and plant. It was easier if he was around during the day to help out if there were any problems and then he could learn at his own pace too, catching up for missed school work at irregular hours that fitted his schedule.

At lunch we walked home because it had warmed up a bit. We had another great lunch, and the house was filled with the sounds of laughter. For the time being I could forget my haunting dreams, I was actually happy for a while, and I found out that at most times surrounded by our new friends and my family I could be happy, it was at night that trouble arose.

That evening as we sat by their gas fireplace Mom asked Lucy about the snow.

"Does it stay all year?"

"No," Lucy replied "It won't stay; it'll be gone in a week or two. It normally only starts to stick around the start of November." Or so she thought. It ended up staying from then until mid-May, so the only glimpse of the grass we would get for now, was on the night we had flown into Toronto.

My earlier worries seemed to prove right. That night when I lay down to sleep home sickness engulfed me. I tried to brush it away with the thoughts of the great day but it kept crashing down on me. When I finally got to sleep it would only be for about thirty minutes before another nightmare shook me out of slumber. The nights were more tiring for me than the busiest day we had had in Canada so far. I woke up shivering around two-thirty and I crawled out of bed, to a chair in between my parent's room and mine. I curled up in the chair and tucked my feet up, hugging my knees, hoping that if I squeezed tight enough I could hold myself together. I clutched my chest again as another wave of pain racked through me. I closed my eyes, trying to dispel the images of the war vets and concentrated on Mom and Dad's breathing, timing my breath with theirs. *Breathe in, breathe out, breathe in, breathe out.* Suddenly I heard Mom wake up in their room with a gasp.

"You okay Mom?" I whispered anxiously.

"Yeah, fine thanks. Why are you still awake?" She asked me as she padded out of the room, over to me.

"Well…" I replied, trying to think of an excuse.

"Couldn't sleep either?"

I nodded.

"That's okay, want to tell me what it was about?"

I shrugged.

Mom sighed and came to sit on the edge of my chair. We talked for a while about this and that, avoiding the subject of nightmares and Zimbabwe. Eventually Mom sighed.

"We should get some sleep; otherwise we won't be able to wake up tomorrow." She said, grinning weakly at me. I smiled back and crossed over to my room, lying down and snuggling into the soft folds of the bed.

I concentrated on deepening my breathing, when that didn't work I tried counting sheep. That didn't work for me either, but maybe it was because when I would start dozing off the sheep would start turning evil and repeating, "I'll get you!" over and over. Next I tried slowly concentrating on each part of my body and relaxing it. By the time I finished from my head to my toes, I lay limp in the bed. Slowly I drifted into a deep sleep. I'm not sure whether it was because I had used up all the scary memories my tired brain could pull to the fore front of my mind, or if it was just that I was too tired to remember them at the moment but for the first time since we had arrived in Canada, I slept well.

When I woke up late the next morning I smelt frying eggs and heard the sizzling of bacon. I inhaled deeply and exhaled, mmmm. I clambered out of bed and up the stairs, still in a daze, drawn by the appealing smells of breakfast.

"Morning sleepy head!" Gary said smiling over at me.

"Morning." I mumbled as Gary neatly slipped the bacon onto a plate and set it down in front of me. I had arrived just in time for breakfast. Gary slid into his seat and smiled. After we had said thanks for our food we dug in. The only sounds you could hear for the first few Moments were the sounds of cutlery on plates. After everyone had gobbled up the first bit of their breakfast the usual morning banter started.

Later after everything was cleared up Lucy and Gary scratched up some old mittens and winter coats for us. Luke and I rushed outside and looked at the abundance of white fluffy snow all around us. I fell down into a shallow snow bank and was rewarded with a dump of snow down my back. I yelled out and got hit with a snow ball. James had come out to join us.

"Hey!" I screeched back in surprise. I picked up two handfuls of snow and packed it together. It was kind of rough but for my first time it wasn't bad and I figured it was going to go splat as soon as it hit him anyways. I fired my snowball back at him and laughed in satisfaction when it splattered down the front of his coat. Not bad for my first try! In a moment of glory from my last throw I scooped up an armful of snow and made eight snowballs. I then began pelting Luke and James alike. They retreated about ten feet and looked at each other. They nodded and both scooped up loads of snow. I started making walls for a fort; much to my disappointment there wasn't enough snow to do more than a fifteen centimetre wall, the snow really wasn't that deep. James and Luke had found out that there wasn't enough snow left to make more than a few snowballs. We shrugged at each other and bombarded each other with the snowballs we had already made.

We came in about fifteen minutes later covered in snow and ice, laughing our heads off. Mom took one look at us and burst into laughter too. It was only minus twelve but it was twice as cold as the coldest we had ever been and having been out there for over twenty minutes was a huge feat for a Zimbabwean. Mom couldn't believe that we had stayed out so long and neither could I. The day slid by quickly as had the past few days. None of the past four days since we had arrived had held too much important content. We would start house hunting as soon as Mom and Dad talked to their lawyer and the bank. We hoped that we would be able to get a down payment on the house at least. Gary and Lucy assured us that there was no hurry; they didn't mind having us stay with them. We were overwhelmed with their continuous generosity and kindness. They gave so much and asked for nothing in return.

The next day was Sunday. We went to a little gathering not too far from Gary and Lucy's house. When we got back we had a delicious lunch of chicken, mashed potatoes, buns and apple turnovers for dessert. I leaned back, content for the moment. How could it be that at times I was so happy, but that one wrong thought sent me into the deep abyss of homesickness? How would I be able to ever explain it to someone else who wasn't in my mind, when I wasn't even able to explain it to myself?

"Hey, what's on your mind?" Luke asked me later that evening. I shrugged, unable to come up with the words to express how I felt. If there was anyone I could tell it would be Luke or Mom, but most likely Luke, because we were a little closer in age and we had a better understanding of each other.

"Hey, its okay, I understand. It's hard, especially for you and me right now, but we just have to believe that it will get easier, and help each other out." Luke said softly.

I smiled at him in admiration, he was considerate and always looking out for me, even when he was just as bad or worse off than I was. He was everything I wanted to be and we got along really well, we hardly ever fought. We chatted for a while, just about this and that until the doorbell rang. Gary answered the door and outside in the falling snow stood 'miss wiggly hips'.

I stood behind Gary glaring at her. She looked embarrassed, her face red she averted her eyes from me and looked at Gary.

"Uh," she muttered, "I'm here to talk to Josh, and Lannette." She kept her eyes on the ground as she spoke.

Gary looked at her in confusion; I remembered that he hadn't seen my outburst. "I'll check with them, one minute, but come on in its chilly out there."

She stumbled over the words as she thanked him, and took the two steps it took to get in the doorway. Gary walked away with a glance between the two of us. Mom walked up with a wary looking Dad close behind her. Dad cast me a look as if to say 'look at what you've done!' I didn't lower my gaze but rather felt a little bit disgruntled, I knew I really shouldn't have yelled at her but at the same time I still felt that she had deserved every word of my speech.

"Uh, I'm here just to say that I'm sorry and that I won't do it again. I wasn't thinking and…" Her voice faltered awkwardly.

"We… Understand," Dad said, cautiously looking at Mom. "We were upset about what happened but Thomas didn't have the right to yell at you either." He looked at me pointedly clearly wanting me to apologize. I gave him a quick sharp look but he missed it.

"I'm… Sorry." I said grudgingly.

"That's fine, you were kind of right and I would have done what you did as well…Probably." She gave me a sheepish grin. I smiled haltingly back at her.

"It was nice of you to come by." Mom added. I smiled; well that was one more thing off of my mind. I didn't think that we would have too much more trouble from 'miss wiggly hips'. I supposed I would learn her name a little later on but for now I would keep calling her that as she still walked around shaking her hips like a super model trying to put her hip out of place. How she didn't put her hip out of place is beyond me.

"Why don't we try and start again?" 'Miss wiggly hips' suggested. "Welcome to Canada, my name is Alexi."

"Pleased to meet you, this is my wife Lannette and my oldest child Luke, my other son Thomas and little Katelyn. Mom glanced once at Dad and then shook hands with Alexi.

Tortured nights

That night I had another good night of sleep. I slept soundly and woke up the next morning feeling refreshed. I lay in bed a while after I woke and thought of the past two weeks. Fond memories of Gary and Lucy, as well as the not so good, like the awkward silences of the night Alexi came to apologize. There had also been a few silent dinners when one little thing had been mentioned that sent someone into silence. Normally it was Mom or Luke. I had been one of the silent ones once or twice, but I'd learned how to hide it pretty well now. I banished the mundane thoughts and hopped out of bed.

Lucy had breakfast on the table when I opened the door from the stairs leading into the open kitchen/dining room. Every one glanced at me before returning to their breakfast.

"Morning hon. Sorry we started without you but you were sleeping so soundly we didn't want to disturb you," Mom explained.

"It's fine." I said unperturbed as I slid into my seat. James passed me the toast and eggs. All eyes were on me as I dished up some breakfast for myself.

"Uh, something up?" I questioned, raising my eyebrows.

"No." Luke smirked.

"Okay, seriously. What's up?" I pressed them, my curiosity piqued.

"We were just thinking about the day." Mom assured me. "We had discussed going to the bank today, because as you know we are going to request a loan for a house and hopefully a car. Lucy has offered to go down and testify that we will pay the bills, which might help convince the bank to give us a loan." Mom finished with a grateful smile at Lucy.

"Oh, sounds like fun." I replied, shoveling food into my mouth. The past two weeks had passed in a familiar blur of doing nothing, so a change would be nice. We would be getting plenty of change soon enough though, as we started school on the following Monday. I only hoped that most of the change would be good. I knew that starting at a new school wasn't always fun, and could be quite trying sometimes.

As we climbed into the car later we all wore smiles. We had gotten lucky with the bank and we had been given a loan. It had taken a good part of the morning to get it, though it was much faster than going to the bank in Africa would have been. In Africa you could wait all day just to be seen to, and then you still had to work through the negotiations and work out how it was going to happen.

It was Friday and the last free week day before we started school. Lucy came with Mom and I to get some school supplies. We didn't know what Luke and I would need; so Lucy just made a list of what you most regularly needed. We bought all the basic things we would need, like paper, pencils and binders. Mom looked around for snowsuits too. They were quite expensive, but essential to living in Canada in the winter. We had also been expecting a little time to get organized, and then buy snowsuits. We definitely hadn't been ready for snow two days after we arrived.

Dad later asked Gary if we could help pay for food or

something, Gary just replied that entertainment had to be worth something. Dad didn't know whether to laugh or cry. We must have been pretty good entertainment though; because in between the spaghetti eating contests - including getting it behind our ears and down our shirts - we lost our dignity and just didn't bother being neat and careful, but gained a few laughs in the process. Gary showed us a few gimmicks he had for pranks and jokes. I was seven and Luke was eight going on nine, so we didn't worry too much about what they thought; and it didn't matter anyway - they loved us for who we were, eating contests and all. Gary and Lucy's dog, Jill was a lot of fun to play with in the snow; she would jump all over and chase after the snowballs that we would throw.

Dad had started work; and for the past few days I had gone to work with him, Gary and occasionally James. It was more fun than you might think, and there was always something going on somewhere. Mom was also going to start working soon, as she would be starting just a few days after we started school. She would only be working part time because of Katelyn.

I had gotten a few good nights sleep now and I would find out that it was a good thing because I wouldn't be getting too many more of them for a while; that night the nightmares started again.

I was laughing and climbing up the jungle gym with Luke right on my heels. Our maid Rosemary was watching us and smiling. I jumped down in the middle of a box, and then started pulling myself through the twisted bars. We were laughing so hard that Luke slipped but caught himself at the last second. This only caused us to laugh even harder as we ran away from Mom.

We had been chasing Mom with a frog but now the tables were turned and she was chasing us. We had been closing in on her when we slipped in the wetgrass. Luke was holding the frog and it slipped out of his hands, right down Mom's shirt. Mom started hopping up and down screaming her head off. The servants had all come running as fast as they could; seemingly expecting Mom was being strangled by some murderer. Mom hadn't been sure whether to yell at us or laugh and chase us around the playground area. We hadn't given her time to decide, we just turned and ran. Mom had decided to follow us.

Now she ran along, just behind us and closing in fast. It's amazing how fast she could run when she wanted to. We laughed and kept running until we were so out of breath we fell down in a heap. One of our coal black kittens ran up to see what all the noise was about. I scooped her up and she started to purr. Mom crawled over and stroked her as well.

"I'm going to…" she murmured quietly, not wanting to startle the playful kitten. The rest was lost amidst the rumbling being emitted from the kitten's chest.

Gun shots echoed across the yard, making us all jump. Yells reached us and Mom leapt up in flurry of action she pulled Luke and I up, called for our caretaker and maid Rosemary and dashed for the house. I scooped up the kitten and ran hot on their heels. Rosemary had Katelyn and handed her to Mom as we scurried in the door. Mom locked the door and ran for Dad's shotgun beside his bed as the gates swung open. We watched from the barred windows and wondered what could have happened. We had hired guards and we had a huge fence, but they had still gotten in. It should have been impossible, but it had happened, our worst fear was coming true. The guard dogs charged at the war vets, teeth bared. The war vets didn't even hesitate; they pulled their guns up and shot with their semi - automatics, our dogs fell. Two of the guards from out front had obviously survived and they ran in now and opened fire. Mom helped from the window. Mom was gentle and hated fighting. I knew how much this cost her to have to use her skills as a gunman. Just as Mom was reloading a face appeared at the window and peered in from behind the bars. His foul breath blew over us.

"We're looking for Mr.Mafeotzy!" *The gravelly voice barked.*

Then it all changed.

We were standing in the shop with the same guy standing in front of us, glaring around, his gun held up, as if he was ready to shoot. Mom just stared at him with utter distaste and distrust.

"I don't know where he is!" *She stated bluntly raising her chin.*

"Humph!" *He said and then Mom fell, a gaping bullet hole parting her chest.*

"Mom!"

Next was Luke, still trying to protect Katelyn.

"No!"

I tried to step in front of the bullet that was imminently headed for her forehead, but the bullet moved quicker.

"Katelyn! No, no, no, no, no, no! Katelyn!"

The guy stopped then and announced.

"If you tell us where your Dad is maybe we'll let you live." I knew he was lying, he would kill both Dad and I, if I told him. Besides it wouldn't be worthwhile to live while the rest of your family was killed. None of us had ever done anything wrong, they only wanted to see Dad so that they could kill him and take our land!

"Never!"

"Then you can die too!" *he said his eyes cold.* "We'll find him anyways! Last chance…"

"I'd rather die a hundred times you stupid…!" I couldn't think of the words to describe how stupid he was.

"Then die you shall!" *he proclaimed loudly and he pulled the trigger. It seemed to happen in slow motion. I could have ducked but I forced my instinct to the back of my mind and instead remained in the line of the bullet. Pain tore at my chest and then all went dark.*

Nightmares come to life

I woke up, jolting upright, my back as straight and taut as a board. I drew in a ragged breath, pain still bloomed in my chest and for a moment I was still in the dream, captured by the sight of blood pooling around me. Then the pain faded and I got a chance to fully escape the horror of my nightmare. It felt like the picture of my family falling was imprinted onto my eyelids. I crept out of bed and down the hall, careful not to make any noise and wake up everyone else. The house was eerily quiet without the laughter and conversation that normally filled it.

I realized that without anyone else awake the house was strangely frightening. My recent nightmare didn't help with those thoughts, and at every corner a war vet loomed over me. Every shadow was one waiting to pounce on me. I went and sat down looking around from the corner of my eye. Then my irrational fear suddenly wasn't that irrational. I heard footsteps heading my way. I was paralyzed with fear, unable to hide and protect myself. They drew closer and I slipped out of my stupor, leaping up in a flurry of action. I quickly but silently darted under the pull out couch in the main part of the downstairs living area. The footsteps continued to come.

The person paused and then started for the bed. I

remembered being told once that movement caught your eye so I pressed myself down onto the ground and lay as still as I could, barely daring to breathe. The stranger stopped, and then the footsteps started away, the padding of feet echoed across the room reverberating in my ears. They started for the room that Mom and Dad slept in and quietly opened the door. They crept in silently.

"Josh, Josh!" I heard them whisper in the quiet of the early hours. I was freezing pressed against the floor but I didn't dare move for fear of being caught. I should have realized that no strange intruder would have gone and woken Dad but I was over tired, scared and still half in my dream. I saw the intruder appear back in the doorway and they peered around suspiciously. In my confused state I decided that I wouldn't let them harm my family. I rolled out from under the couch and started running towards the intruder, spurred on by the need to defend my family.

"No!" I cried out in spite of myself. In the faint light that was coming in the window from the moon, I saw the intruder turn to see me bearing down on them. They raised their hands and I thought I saw the faint outline of a gun being raised up. They started to say something but I barreled into them, slamming them to the ground in a wild tackle. Dad came running to the door, suddenly wide awake. I struggled with the stranger on the floor yanking their hands behind their back in the self - defense I had needed to learn in Africa. In some ways when I looked back on the experience, I was still half way in dreamland even though I felt wide awake with the adrenaline running in my veins, pumping along with my furious heartbeat. Dad yanked me off of the person roughly shaking me.

"What do you think you're doing Thomas? Have you gone crazy? Why in the world are you beating up your mother?" Dad was very protective and loving of Mom and this made him extremely angry. He stared at me with a wild fury in his eyes as if he couldn't even believe what I had been doing. In a way neither could I.

"It's not Mom, they were going to kill you, and they were trying to kill you!" I cried almost in frenzy. Dad slapped me across the cheek, not hard but just to try and jolt me out of whatever crazy state I was in. I started to sob uncontrollably.

"It isn't Mom, it isn't Mom! They're going to kill us, they're going to kill us!" I repeated over and over amidst sobs. "They killed Mom, Luke, and Katelyn, then me because I wouldn't tell them where you were. They were looking for you to kill you too! They followed us here and now they're going to kill us all!" I was shaking all over now and I sank to the floor unable to hold up my own weight. I quivered at Moms touch and then completely went over the edge, if I hadn't been there before.

"They're going to kill us Mom! Look out! Run, hide! They're going to kill us!"

"Shh, Shh, hush now Thomas, It's alright, we're here now, it's alright!"

"No it's not! Look, look he got away but he'll be back, just wait! Look he's gone, but he'll be back! He's hunting us! He's going to kill us just like he killed us in Africa! He's going to kill us!" I ranted on and on.

"Thomas you're dreaming, you were dreaming! We didn't die in Africa! Thomas, Thomas!" I wept into her shoulder like a baby. I was so far gone into my nightmare that I couldn't feel ashamed.

"He's gone completely crazy!" Dad said quietly to Mom. "He attacked you and now he's going on about dying, and this guy trying to kill us!" Dad had sometimes joked about me being crazy before, but I knew he wasn't joking now.

"I'm not crazy! He was walking around and I hid under

the pull out couch! I know I shouldn't have but I did! I hid because I was scared!" My eyes started playing tricks on me, and it was like I was still dreaming. I saw him sneaking up on us from behind, gun in hand, this time I was certain I was right. It was too real to be a dream or just my imagination.

"Look! There he is! He's coming, He's coming! Dad run get your gun, wake Luke do something, he's going to kill us!" I started shivering uncontrollably again. Dad picked me up and carried me back to bed. Mom felt my forehead.

"He's got a raging fever." She said and walked quickly out of the room to go and look in the medicine case for something to bring it down.

I slipped into a fitful sleep, tossing and turning. I didn't really dream as such again, but my mind replayed the earlier nightmare scenes of Mom, Luke and Katelyn falling again, and again. In the morning my fever still hadn't gone down much and I slept most of the day. Lucy had to work but she took Mom into town to get some more medicine for me. The next day was much the same and Mom and Dad were afraid that they would have to delay my return to school. As it turned out though I started a quick recovery on the third day and was able to get up and move around by the fourth day, almost back to normal. By the time the weekend ended I was all rested and ready for school.

When I had first fully awakened from my restless slumber on the third day I had seen the bruises that I had inflicted on Mom and was distraught at what I had done to her. Dad decided that even in my sickened state I had taken things too far and that I needed to go with Mom when she next went to talk to the therapist. He said they wouldn't force me to go if I seemed to be doing okay, but I would have to go for at least two weeks, with two sessions a week. As it turned out I ended going for up to a month before they decided they wouldn't force me to go anymore. It didn't seem to be helping me a much anyways. There was some benefit from it, but not as much as they would have hoped. I still had frequent nightmares. We always wondered how much of the sickness had actually been the reason for my delusional seeing of things. I knew personally that it had only been part of it.

After the incident where I started strangling Mom I only had three more 'sightings' of the leader of the war vets. I still believed for quite a while though that he was out there stalking me, waiting for the right Moment to pounce and obliterate us. Mom worried consistently about me after I stopped going to the psychiatrist, always afraid that I might crack again. Dad promised Mom that he would keep an eye on me, and he did. I always felt ashamed of what I had done, and felt like I had betrayed their trust in me. For a while I wondered if I was almost as bad as the war vets, and if maybe I was actually crazy. I had tried to kill my own mother, for crying out loud! The worst part was that it was all done in the belief that I was protecting my Mom and the rest of my family. I didn't believe I could be truly sane if I was doing stuff like that. As for the 'sightings' they just reinforced my belief that I was half mad. Mom assured me many a time that it was just my mind still trying to catch up with all that had happened, and it wasn't truly my fault, but how could I believe her? I felt as if I didn't even know myself, so how could I believe that she would know me well enough to truly believe that.

New school, new struggles

I started school on Monday as promised and most of it lived up to my fears. I walked into the grade three classroom with my backpack of things and the coat that Mom and Dad had bought for me. The teacher was very kind and introduced me to the class. Of course, as most kids do I dreaded standing up there all alone while everyone stared at me. The teacher asked me to tell a little bit about myself. I wasn't quite sure what to say so I looked at the ground and stuttered out.

"I'm from Zimbabwe, I just moved here and my name is Thomas." I kept scrutinizing the floor in my embarrassment and then fell silent, feeling very insignificant and small.

"That's very interesting! Imagine being from Zimbabwe!" said the teacher, thankfully drawing some of the attention away from me, if but for just a moment.

"Where's Zimbabwe?" One kid piped up from the third row. This prompted outbursts from the other children.

"Are you really from that place? What if you're lying?" That one made me really angry. What reason did I have for lying? I looked up and glared in the general direction the comment had come from.

"You talk really funny!" *Ouch!* Well I knew that it wasn't me who was talking funny, but my new classmates. I had spoken normally for my whole life and I was speaking normally now.

"You need to be kind to Thomas he's gone through quite a lot and there's no need for you to talk to him that way!" The teacher said interrupting the other cries. "Of course he's not lying about being from Zimbabwe, Zimbabwe is in Africa, and he probably thinks you talk funny! He's from a different country so it will take some getting used to for him! I expect you to all be respectful and kind!" She continued looking at each of them fiercely. This made me feel even more embarrassed because now they would all be upset with me for getting them into trouble. I hoped that the rest of the day would pick up a bit.

Mrs.Langstaff - as I learned her name was - partnered me up with a boy named Randy to show me around and help me get settled in. We found out that we had a lot in common and hit it off as good friends. For now, he was everything I had wanted as a friend to help me get over my homesickness. His birthday was the day after mine and we had most of the same interests. He showed me where I could keep my things and then helped me get used to the class schedule. School started at nine o'clock and the final bell was at three. We had two classes each forty - five minutes long before a break. The other kids called it recess and I soon picked up the name. At recess Randy led me to the back of the room to get our coats, snow pants, gloves and all the other necessities for the winter wonderland outside. He then led the way to the door at the end of the passage.

Only then, he explained could we pull on our boots, because they didn't want the floor getting all dirty. Kids mingled all around us, talking, and laughing. I pulled on my boots and raced out after Randy. The playground was grand. At one end it had a dome thing made out of bars. Randy told me it was an igloo; he then of course had to inform me on what an igloo was. Randy led the way over to a group of boys from our class. I followed obediently behind him. For an awkward minute or so the boys just stood there staring at me. I shifted my weight to the other foot, quite unsettled by their unwavering gaze.

"Okay, seriously, are you really from that place in Africa? I hate to say it but I find that really hard to believe. Even If you were from that place why would you leave there? It must have been awesome!" blurted out one of the boys.

I wasn't sure whether he thought it was cool if I was from Africa or if he didn't believe me, and was mad at me because he thought I was lying.

"Yes, I'm honestly from Africa. We left because we had to; we didn't really have a choice."

"How could someone force you to leave your home?" Another boy spoke up, also disbelieving.

"You're just lucky you don't know!" I shot back getting upset as an onslaught of memories blocked up my mind.

"What's that supposed to mean?" The first boy spoke up challenging me now.

"It means I was held at gun point! I was threatened at gun point and forced to leave my home" I said angrily.

"Honestly? I doubt it! Yeah right, you were not held at gun point! Like they could do that to you and get away with it!" spoke up the third boy.

"Actually they can, and they did! Just because you've never left this country, where maybe they couldn't, doesn't mean that in other places it doesn't happen! It does and I know that personally!" I couldn't believe that they didn't believe me. How would they know anyways?

"Hey, maybe he is telling the truth." Said the first boy. "I mean, why would he lie?"

"He isn't lying, its true!" Randy confirmed. This seemed to put their minds at ease for the Moment and we stood in silence for a while. The bell rang and the boys charged for the line ups that were forming in front of the doors. I followed suit hastily, not wanting to be left behind. I ran up behind Randy just as the line-up started to move into the school.

As the day moved on I got quite a few jabs about my accent and some of the Shona words I mixed in with my English. I had never noticed it before because we had all spoken like that; I had been no different than anybody else, but now I was. I started to get upset when every time I spoke people sniggered, snickered and giggled behind my back. One time someone started to openly guffaw not even trying to disguise his laughter. I turned around and glared at him so ferociously that he stopped and looked down at his work.

I had always been a bright student that got straight A's. I knew most of the answers but eventually I stopped putting up my hand because every time I did I was made fun of. There were some things that I didn't know because the curriculums in Africa were different; I talked to the teacher after every class about the work I didn't know - at her request. Mrs. Langstaff assured me that I would catch up soon enough, and shouldn't have too much trouble.

When the bell rang around lunch time I walked out into the corridor, gathered my things and went to wait at the doors. People milled all around me, but none of them had their coats on. I ignored this fact for a while and instead scanned the throng of people for Luke. We had said that we would meet here for Mom to pick us up. He showed up in a few minutes. By now everything had calmed down some, but most people had just gone back into the classroom.

"Looks like they get out even earlier here, awesome!" Luke commented. I had heard a few Canadians using that expression and it seemed Luke had picked up on it mighty quick!

"You know," I started, "That phrase sounds kind of funny when you say it with your accent!"

"What accent good fellow?" Luke said using his silliest British accent. "I mean it's everyone else that has the accent, what what?" We burst out laughing and everyone else in the hallway turned to stare at us. A lot of noises were coming from down the passage which Randy had indicated was the 'auditorium'. We went to go and see what was happening. It looked like all the older kids from forms seven to twelve were gathered there, eating lunch and chatting away. I thought maybe they had some sort of meeting and were possibly allowed to eat while they waited. Luke led me back down the passage to where we had been waiting before, explaining that Mom should be here any minute.

We waited and waited, but Mom didn't show up. A second bell rang and everyone poured into the hall ways, got dressed and headed outside. We figured it must be home time now and maybe we had missed a short home room class by mistake. Randy came looking for me and asked me what I was waiting for. I explained that I was waiting for my Mom to pick us up. He looked at me curiously.

"Where were you at lunch?"

"We didn't know you guys have lunch before you go home." I said.

"What do you mean Thomas? Aren't you feeling good? Why are you going home?"

"Oh, don't you all?"

"All what?" Randy asked, obviously as confused as I was.

"All go home at lunch time." Luke interrupted.

"I wish! Didn't you know? We have lunch and then recess. After Recess we come back in for two more classes. We then have another short recess before our last class. School goes until three fifteen. Wait do you mean to tell me that you used to get out from school at lunch in Zem... Zumbew... Africa!"

"Yes, we thought you did everywhere. That must be an extremely long day, to have school all day long. When do you play? You wouldn't have much time before it got too cold and dark outside!" I exclaimed.

"School! All day!" Luke sputtered out appalled. "I don't think I could stand school all day long!"

"Well, you better get used to it and quick because that's the way it is!" Randy said and led us back down the passage way.

When we got to the class room we found that Mom had packed us lunch. We thought that it was meant for a snack, now we realised why she had packed it. I felt like such an idiot.

Mrs.Langstaff allowed me to stay in and eat my lunch. By the time I had finished there wasn't much time left to go out and play. Instead Randy led me around and showed me a bit more of the school. The library was on the second level, up where most of the high school classrooms were. I found out that there was a pre-school way down a long 'hall way' - as the Canadians called it - and we walked past the cafeteria that was beside the auditorium. A few high school kids still lingered, finishing up their lunches. The cafeteria still had the smell of whatever it was that they had been serving for lunch that day, I didn't know what it was, but it smelled good!

When the bell rang we headed back to the grade three classroom. As I settled back into my desk I felt someone put something on my back. I turned around and took the sign off of my back. I glared around at the people behind me.

"Who put this on my back?" I asked my voice dangerously quiet.

"I did, what are you going to do about it?" A boy named

Rylie said smiling smugly. I got out of my seat and calmly walked down the aisle to his desk.

"Don't do that again!" I said and put it on his desk. I stood there for a minute staring at him. He looked away, not as smug. I turned and walked back to my seat.

"He's so stupid!" I heard him whisper behind my back. I spun around.

"If you're too cowardly to say that to my face then why say it at all?" I spat out, my eyes narrowed.

"If you're too cowardly to say that to my face..." Rylie mimicked in a girly voice.

"Oh there you go again. I believe the kindergarten classroom is down the hall Rylie." I said back smiling sweetly.

Ryle's posse stared at me, Rylie stood up.

"Are you calling me stupid?" He asked, now on the defensive.

"I didn't call anyone anything, but I just thought that the kindergarten classroom is where you belong because I believe that's where the high voiced mimicking thing was last cool." I replied venomously.

"Listen, Tom-weirdo you can just go back to where ever you came from and if you don't go by yourself I'll punch you all the way there!" Rylie threatened, stepping up and pushing his face up against mine.

"How could you? You're too dumb to know where it is." I asked, getting fed up now.

"I can find a map!" Rylie spat at me.

"But that might require reading, maybe you should get one of your posse to do it for you since you can't!" I replied.

Rylie stood there for a moment that stretched for an eternity in my mind. He was dumbfounded that he had been stood up to. He was used to getting his way, but nobody was going to push me around. Finally Rylie spun around and sat down heavily in his seat.

I walked back to my desk and received a round of pats on the back from a few of my classmates, mostly guys. Mrs. Langstaff walked into the room just as I slid into my seat. I smiled thankfully that she hadn't come in just a few minutes before because Rylie and I had come close to blows, my parents wouldn't have been impressed with me being sent to the headmasters office on the first day of school.

Christmas Peace

In the next two weeks we went around looking at houses. It didn't take long to find one and we moved into our new house within a month and a half of arriving in Canada. It was a Friday when we moved in. We hadn't known anyone when we had arrived but now we had quite a few friends and they all pitched in to help us settle. The next day the real estate lady came to help us unpack but found a lot of it already done.

"I thought you didn't know anyone when you came here." She commented while helping Mom unpack some silverware.

"We didn't, we met them at..." Mom wasn't quite sure how to explain it, "our gathering, a little bit like church."

"They came and helped? I thought you just met them."

"Yes they're very kind people." Mom replied smiling softly.

It didn't take us long to settle in and we were given many things by our new friends. Our new house was only two or three blocks from our school too, so when it was warm enough, we could just walk to school, which was a bonus.

Things started moving forward in life again and I continued with school, falling into a routine of school, ride the bus to the plant and then home again when Mom was ready. Luke and I would play with Gary and Lucy's dog Jill, in the snow until we got cold, tired, or it got too dark.

In the flurry of activity that surrounded me for about two months; starting school, settling into our new house and such, it was easy to forget where I was and why. Rylie didn't cause too much trouble after our stand off and I was making some good friends. At night the nightmares slowed and I got more rest. Every now and then they would rear their big ugly heads and leave me sitting up and shaking in bed, but apart from that, I was adjusting quickly to my new life.

One particular nightmare woke me up one night. I was still inclined to forget where I was sometimes, even though we'd been living in our new house for a while. I looked around my room at the few things that filled it up. I had the few toys I'd brought with in a corner, my bed in the other and a few other things sitting beside my closet. We hoped to be able to get a bedroom set later on, but for now we had to build the foundation of our new life style. It was hard for Mom and Dad to have to restart their life, at this age.

Life continued in the new routine. Mom and Dad were working hard trying to keep up with the bills that were starting to flow in. Luke and I helped, but I have to admit that we were preoccupied with our own lives at that point. Later on, when I looked back, I felt bad that we hadn't tried to help Mom and Dad more because it was a really tough time for them, and I'm sure they would have appreciated more help from us.

Time passed and we became more accustomed to the weather. Christmas was starting to approach and it seemed entirely different with snow covering the ground. We all started getting ready for Christmas break and making plans. I hoped to visit Randy's house over the holidays because we weren't going to be doing much. We were planning to visit

Gary and Lucy on Christmas day and we were going to visit some other friends, Ted and Alice, for New Year's Eve.

Mom and Dad had warned us not to expect too much. Of course by this time we had given up our belief in Santa, so Mom and Dad cautioned us that they might not be able to afford to get us any of the things we were used to receiving on Christmas morning. Traditionally as a family we would exchange a few gifts and spend a nice day at home or visiting our grandparents. Of course now it would have been an extremely long journey to visit them this year. Mom was starting to get really emotional, and it affected me too. Even Dad and Luke seemed glum. Katelyn felt the mood change too, and she got cranky and cried a lot. It became apparent that Christmas in our family had been all about spending time with our relatives and family. Christmas loomed over us and it really didn't seem as important any more, just knowing that we wouldn't be seeing Grandma and Grandpa this year. Around this time my nightmares flared once more. I started getting less sleep again and this affected my mood. I wasn't super happy in the first place so I was really depressed by the time Christmas holidays came around.

On the last day of school my class mates milled all around me getting their coats on and talking excitedly.

"We really have to get together over the holidays!" Randy said to me over the hubbub. I smile in agreement and nodded my head.

"Definitely! If you'll give me your phone number I'll give you a call!" I replied, but most of my answer was lost in the clamour made by a bunch of excited kids. Randy must have heard some of it and understood what I meant because he scrounged up a piece of scrap paper and jotted down his number. We broke out of the mass of kids fighting towards the door, and freedom. I managed to get my boots on while being shoved by the older kids struggling to get out of the door. Randy and I said our farewells and split off in different directions.

When we arrived at the plant Mom and Dad were struggling with the plants computer server. It had crashed, and they had to try and get it back up again. It started getting late in the afternoon but Mom and Dad weren't anywhere near being done. By early evening it was clear that Mom and Dad were going to be a while. Gary and Lucy offered to take us to their home for now. We walked across to their house and Lucy started spaghetti for supper. This started a chain for many more spaghetti eating contests. After we had eaten dinner, Lucy carried some spaghetti across for Mom and Dad and I was once again humbled by their generosity.

Mom and Dad were still working when we left the plant after giving them their supper, so we ended up staying the night at Gary and Lucy's. We did this a couple of times, after this first instance, and we always had a lot of fun. Sometimes on the weekends we'd go and stay there too. If they ever minded having us over they definitely didn't show it in anyway. The Christmas holidays weren't exactly filled with activity and I ended up spending most of the time at the office, not that I minded. I loved going to the office. We had a lot of fun outside and inside. We would go around the plant and talk to the other people working there and make paper cup stacks. We found all kinds of games to play and had tons of fun.

It turned out that Randy was visiting his Grandparents for most of the holiday so we decided to hang out another time. On Christmas morning Luke and I went downstairs and found a few presents in the corner of the living room. In the afternoon we found our other surprise. We had had a lot of pets in Africa and we missed them a lot so we were getting a cat. Because we lived in town we couldn't get a big dog, so we thought we might start out with a kitten. We traveled a little ways and came to a house. Dad looked at Mom and she nodded. Dad pulled into the driveway and parked the car. We all climbed out and walked to the door. Dad rang the doorbell and someone walked up to the door. Once we got past all of the pleasantries the man led us to an outside cat house. It was heated by a small floor heater and they had plenty of toys all over the room. There were quite a few little kittens running around our feet.

"Take your pick." The man offered, and stepped back to let us in. Luke and I looked at all the kittens and picked up a few of them. One of the kittens purred every time we picked him up or stroked him. Mom didn't want a female cat so we asked the man which ones were females and which ones were males. That helped narrow it down to about three little fluff balls. We decided on the one that purred all the time but also loved to play with his other brothers and sisters.

We had brought a cardboard box that we put him in and settled him down in the soft blankets. He started mewling as soon as the car started moving but he soon calmed down and started purring again. The Moment we stopped petting him though, he would start a racket. When we got home we played with him and found a litter box for him. Mom and Dad had hidden it a few days earlier not wanting to spoil the surprise. Over the rest of the Christmas holidays we trained him to use the litter box and played with him. We couldn't take him with us to the plant, but Mom tried to stay home for some of the break, so we spent as much time with him as possible. We also found out one of his quirks. He had no common sense about cars. In the morning when we would want to leave he would try and chase the car, or follow it. After he nearly got run over we decided we couldn't let this continue. One of us would hold Tiger - that's what we named him - while the other one drove out with Mom and shut the garage door. Then we would set him down and run out the front door, locking it behind us. It took a little extra work but we loved him and didn't want him getting run over or hurt.

New Year's came and went and we headed back to school. We had a huge dump of snow a week after we had gone back to school. There was already a lot of snow and it was bitterly cold outside. Nevertheless Luke and I went and played outside. It didn't take much to build a snow fort when all you had to do was go into the front yard and dig a hole. You could pack down the walls and build up the boundaries a little more. All you really had to do was dig a hole in the five foot deep snow. Luke and I had snowball fights too but Luke always won. I was a lot smaller than him and he always beat me. It didn't help that half the time I was bent over roaring with laughter that echoed in the growing darkness. That was another thing that didn't help with depression was the amount of sunlight. The sun would only start to rise when we walked to school, at about eight forty five. The bell rang at nine and it took us about ten minutes to get school. Then we had five minutes to get our things organized for the first few classes. I still got teased a little bit about my accent but within the first few months I had already started to develop a Canadian twang to my usual speech patterns. Mom and Dad didn't change as fast. They said that Luke and I were lucky that we were so young and able to adapt so fast. I hadn't had too much trouble from Rylie besides a few run in's on the playground. Whenever he walked up to taunt me, I coolly ignored him and walked away. I will admit that I didn't exactly try my hardest to make sure I stayed out of trouble. Ignoring him was good but that's about where it ended. He tried to shove me around a bit and I didn't like that, so every time I walked past him, I shoved my shoulder into him and smirked. This infuriated him because he couldn't get back at me by teasing me because I just didn't react. He continued to try to make my life miserable, and I kept at it with an equal vengeance.

It just so happened that we were on the same bus. One particular day had been particularly hard, and Rylie had been driving me to my limits throughout it. The truth is that even though I gave off an air of not caring about what he said, some of the things really struck home and riled me up quite a bit. Rylie tripped me on my way to the door and I went sprawling. I split my lip open and spat out blood. I got up and walked away as if nothing had happened. Rylie was furious. He was sure that I would attack him then and he would have a reason to fight. It wasn't in my nature, though, to just let this go. I acted like I did, but it was far from over. He thought he had won that tiny little battle, but I would make sure he lost the war, or die trying. As I climbed onto the bus Rylie was right behind and I grabbed my chance. I pretended to grab the bar but my hand slid back and I fell back right on top of Rylie. I had planned it of course so I didn't get hurt, but Rylie sure did! As I fell I shoved my sharp elbow out and Rylie felt it hit his gut, hard! As I got up I 'accidently' stepped on his stomach.

"Oh, dear I'm so sorry!" I gasped in false alarm. Rylie must have detected a false note in my tone though, as I tried not to laugh.

"Yeah, sure whatever. I'm sure it was an accident." But his voice was heavy with sarcasm.

"Oh, of course! Absolutely!" I said smiling nicely at him, stopping to pull him. I pulled him up with a jerk, way harder than necessary and made him fall flat on his face again, then clambered onto the bus. When Rylie climbed up a little while later his face was flushed and angry. He shot a death glare at me before slumping in his seat. It wasn't very nice, but I smiled happily all the way home. Revenge is sweet!

Dark days and dark waters

Time passed quickly and my nightmares faded to the back of my mind. We had faced a lot of cold weather and we thought that it was as cold as it could possibly get. We'd had up to, or I suppose down to, minus thirty but in the second week of January we saw our coldest yet. On Thursday morning Dad left for work at seven. He called us shortly after to tell us to listen to the radio before going to school in case the busses weren't running. It turned out that the whole school was closed. We looked at the thermometer outside the window. It was minus forty - eight! It stayed like that for the remainder of the week and two days of the next. It was hard for me to be locked up inside all the time after being so used to running around an open yard.

I could see in small ways that Mom was starting to get depressed. It was easy just to let myself go down with her, but I knew that if I did I wouldn't be able to find my way up again. Mom tried her best to hide it and not let it worry us, but in small ways it was apparent. The old sparkle in her eye was gone, leaving her eyes dull and hollow. Her smiles weren't as frequent and when they did make their appearances, they didn't have the old joy that they used to have. Before the depression Mom's smile would set her glowing. Mom's constant upbeat mood shifted ever so slightly, however when you're balanced on a cliff, when you fall, you fall a long way, and you fall hard. Mom had shifted from the middle of a happy meadow to the edge. She was now balanced on the edge of a cliff, which led to a dark, gloomy sea. When Mom fell off the edge of that cliff her pretences of happiness slowly changed to forced smiles and then, nothing. She lost the will to keep fighting, and to even pretend. She gave herself over for a while and just lay down. She still tried to get up in the mornings and get on with her life, but I could see that something was missing. Mom was a formidable actor. If I hadn't been so close to her I wouldn't have been able to see. When I finally gave up my fight, everyone could see it. The only thing I had the energy to keep up with was my school work. I didn't have the energy to do other things; instead I threw myself into my school work with a vengeance. Besides that I gave up.

Rylie was still sore from what I had done that day getting on the bus, and he did everything he could to get back at me. I didn't respond, but not in the way I had before by ignoring him. Before I had ignored him in a cool, 'I'm not that immature and I'm better than you kind of way, that way I had held my dignity and pride up above his. When I had responded this way I had snubbed him by ignoring him, but now I just let him walk all over me. When he called me names I just slunk away, with my head down in defeat. Rylie smelt blood like a shark and he swooped in to open the wound further. I had a huge emotional cut right now and Rylie widened it as much as possible.

Mom and Dad could see that all wasn't right as I sunk deeper and deeper into the grips of the dark waters of depression. Despair settled over me in a miserable cloud. At some point I stopped caring. I played with our kitten, but not much. I smiled and played with Luke, but not whole heartedly. I ceased to care what Rylie and the other boys called me or said behind my back. I felt empty, hollow, the same as I had seen in Mom.

The funny thing is that after I went down the way Mom had gone, she managed to find the will to climb the cliff she had dropped from. As I fell, she climbed and rose up again. She found a ledge about half way and stayed there for a while. I found her face in my dark struggle in the obscure waters of my own demise. I suppose that without all of the help from friends and family, I would have stayed there, on the brink of survival, just barely living. But as it turned out I found just enough courage to keep going every day. Mom and Dad worried consistently about me. Eventually it was that care that helped me break out of this half living state that I was in. When I watched them looking at me, and talking quietly together, worriedly, I would feel horribly guilty. The small voice in the back of my mind kept penetrating my thoughts and sending awful shots of self - reproach through me.

"As if they need more worry! They have enough to deal with and your Mom is still partially in a bad depression herself!" It whispered.

"You see how they worry about you! You're so selfish sitting around all gloomy. Eventually their frustrations break through and that makes them feel terrible too!"

Even though, I still couldn't manage to work up enough energy to pull myself out of my depression and so time ceased to mean anything to me. I wasn't sure how long I fought against the heavy water that threatened to pull my under but one day I gave up fighting and just let myself slip completely under the waves of despair.

February

March

April

About two weeks before my birthday on April twenty - seventh, Dad stomped into my room where I was lying on my bed, staring up at nothing.

"Your mother and I are worried sick!" he had said. "You're acting so selfish and self - pitying! We're so very privileged to be here and have all that we do! You sit around all gloomy and…And… Well! You help, but so unwillingly. You walk around with your lip on the ground and you're glum all the time. If you can't be nice then just stay here!" He had walked out heated and flushing from anger when I didn't respond, but just looked at him.

Mom cracked from frustration a little while later.

"Do something! You sit around and look at nothing! You depress us all with your attitude! You frustrate your father and me endlessly! What are we supposed to do as we watch you waste away!" She said her voice rising in fury with every word.

I responded to this the same way as Dad's outburst. I stared at her until she sighed and walked out of the room.

The voice in my head later reminded of how resigned they had become after they had had their say. They watched me to see if there was to be a change, but when they didn't see any they seemed to give up. Mom started to sink into depression again. It seemed too much of a coincidence that Mom came out of her depression when I went into mine and when I came out of mine a little while later, she went back into the clutches of hopelessness. We were locked in a wild rollercoaster of depression, but we managed to eventually come out with the wheels still turning. I never went into a bout of depression that serious again.

Life continued, and even though the first day of spring came and went there was no change in the weather. We had another dump of snow on the nineteenth of April and I felt myself slip a little bit into the shallow waters of a new depression. I never got the chance to drown in my sorrows, because slowly but surely, at the end of April signs of spring started to show. The frost on the trees was melting and during the day the sun appeared and shone stronger and warmer. The sun itself was nice but the snow stayed for quite a while yet. A few days before my birthday we caught our first glimpse of grass around the edges of our yard. It was only a few centimetres of grass right along the border but it excited us none the less. It started warming up and on the twenty - first of April it got to a whopping minus twelve! About two weeks after my birthday it started warming up for good.

The thing I noticed when I first came out of the depression was how much things had changed. During my depression my nightmares had started again, and they had left me with a new fear of sleep. It took me ages to get to sleep and I kept waking up in the middle of the night. This made it even harder to keep my head out of the water of darkness - as I grew to think of them. Another thing that had changed was the way that the boys at school looked at me and held me in regard. Rylie had taken advantage of my weakness and turned as many people against me as possible. Fortunately for me Rylie didn't have a ton of followers, beside his posse, so he didn't have much success, but the success he did have was a setback. I hadn't been at school long when I went into my depression so I didn't have much of a reputation yet, but the little I did have was nearly gone. Randy and a few others welcomed me back but a few were grudging. They felt I had deserted them and I supposed that it was partly true. When I went into my depression I failed to do much at school but sit there and do my work. I had mostly ignored their requests to play and such.

Maybe the thing I noticed the most was the amount of time I had spent in my depression. When I first truly 'awakened' and saw the date I thought there was a mistake. It was the twenty - first day of April. I remembered a lot of days passed and going to school and such, but I never dreamed that so much time had passed. I had spent more than three months in my depression and only, finally, banished the last ghost of that depression in the last few days before my birthday. I also remembered the bitter cold and how that had made the depression worse. Many people said that if we had survived this winter we would survive most Canadian winters. Everyone agreed that it was an unusually hard winter.

For my birthday we couldn't throw a huge party but I invited three of my best friends over and had cake and played a few games. Even though it was a small party, my eighth birthday was still special, simply because we were all together and for a while I could stop thinking about what it would have been like in Africa.

When I fell asleep at last that night I returned home, at least in my thoughts.

"Hey, Thomas! Over here!" My best friend, Chris, called out. I smiled at him and started in his direction. We ran towards each other until we were right next to each other. We sat down in the grass and talked; we walked around the yard and went swimming, I was happy to be home.

I jolted out of my dream sweating profusely. I couldn't

understand myself. It was a great dream so why was I so sad? Why did I consider it a bad dream if it reminded me of the good things from home? It was the first time since I'd left Africa that I'd thought of it as home but now I realised that it was true. Canada might be safe and all the things that Mom and Dad kept telling us, but Zimbabwe was still my home. They say that home is where the heart is and it was true. My house in the middle of Bicknell Street, Russell, Manitoba was only a house. For me, my home was where I thought of most often. It was the neighbourhood where my friends lived and it was where my heart stayed. Our farm, an hour outside the capital city of Zimbabwe, was still my home. Even though I had new friends here, my dearest and best friends were the ones that understood me most. All of them still lived at my home, even though I didn't. As these thoughts ran through my head I felt a wave of inexplicable pain rack my body. I gasped at the force of it and sank down deeper in my bed. For a Moment I was un-able to decipher whether it was physical or just emotional pain because the potency of it was so powerful it rendered me helpless for a few Moments. As I lay gasping another memory overtook my mind and transported me to another place and time.

Fanta, our gardener, was washing the car and whistling merrily along in the sunshine. Luke and I were walking towards the play set with Rosemary, our dearest maid that seemed more of a friend, than a servant.

While I dreamed snow started falling outside my window, leaving a new layer of cold snow on the ground. I tossed and turned in my sleep, my mind running through my memories and past. I woke again just a few short hours later. My dreams were both wonderful and excruciating, almost to the point of torture, where I was trapped in my own mind with no escape. Even when I awoke the pain stayed with me. With each fresh surge of pain I felt more and more depressed and it seemed like I would explode from the pent up feelings in my body. Then my world shattered, or at least the little that was still intact did and I was screaming. Screaming from the pain, screaming from my own helplessness, screaming from an agony so great I could no longer withstand it. I screamed for a release from it all, I prayed that it was just a dream, that like my many nightmares this would end and I would be back playing with Rosemary in the garden, chasing Mom with a frog or running through the sprinkler. If it wasn't... Well, I couldn't go there because I didn't know if I could live if it wasn't all just a dream. I started wondering if maybe that would be best, just to die and be free of this hurt. And then it seemed as if my wish had taken place, I had returned home. I hesitated, no, this couldn't be home because the grief was still coursing through my body, and I was still screaming. My scream was no longer from pain. No, now it was fear.

I was sitting at the old computer we had when I heard a noise and turned. Immediately I wished I hadn't. A face leered in at me from the barred window in my room. I opened my mouth to scream but I already was screaming. Now I was confused. Then my thoughts returned to the situation at hand.

"Go away!" I yelled at the man and grabbed the gun from Dad's bedside drawer.

'Wait! I was just in my own room!' My mind cried, but I didn't have time to puzzle over that fact because now the man was in the room with me. A hand touched my shoulder and I heard a far off voice calling my name. I grabbed the gun, aimed and pulled the trigger. Click. Nothing. I had never heard such a foreboding sound in all my life.

'But Dad always kept the gun loaded' my mind bellowed. I reacted on instinct. I raised the gun and began beating on the hand on my shoulder. Then he was dancing around in front of me and I tried to club him again but he was out of reach. I tried again but he leapt out of range again.

As the nightmare faded I tried to grab it and keep it with me but it was twirling just out of my reach just like the war vet had been. It had been a nightmare so why did I want to stay shrouded in it? I knew the answer right away. Because it held pictures of my home. Mom and Dad's room, my own room. All of these things had been in my dream and I wanted to stay there, with them in my mind's eye. Even with the war vet dancing around me I had felt a security there back at home, even though I knew it was foolish. I lay there for what felt like hours just relishing the short glimpses of our home. Then images started flashing in front of my eyes and I couldn't tell if I was awake or asleep. I was aware of my surroundings but all I could see were the memories floating around my head. I swam in our pool, sat on the giant swing in our playground, ran around with my friends in our backyard. I was shaking, not from grief but excitement. I was finally home.

My friends and I sat down with a flop, laughing.

"Long time no see!" I said smiling at all of them, drinking in their faces wishing I could stay there forever. Then again, maybe I could. It seemed too solid, too real to just be a dream. Besides, all of the dreams I'd had so far were nightmares, so I must have woken up from the nightmare I had been living for so long. I laughed again and they rose, walking off. But wait! How could they be walking away? I tried to run after them but couldn't. I felt hopelessness course through me as I struggled. All I knew was that I had to get up, I couldn't let my friends leave without me, I couldn't be alone again.

"Wait!" I yelled but they couldn't hear me. I started sinking into the ground and they didn't even look back. I called out again and again but I still couldn't seem to yell loud enough for them to hear. It started raining and I got soaking wet. The more I thrashed about in the mud the faster I sank. Then I was completely submerged and I was suffocating! Why wouldn't anyone come and help me? I couldn't breathe and it couldn't be

a dream because I started passing out. My friends had left me and I was dying. I couldn't call out and I couldn't move! I sank deeper and deeper but I was still getting wet from the rain. I was sopping wet and choking to death! It was the last thought I had before everything went black.

Bullies and a victory

I woke up confused. How could I wake up when I had died last night? I had just gotten home when I died and it seemed so unfair to me. I had gotten one glimpse of my friends just to have them pulled away from me again in death. My thoughts were all muddled and I couldn't understand it. I heard my name being called. A voice said I was late for school. I came back to the present like a slap across the face. I gasped at the force of the blow. How could I have been so sure that it was true, how could it have been so real and yet a dream? I felt betrayed by my own mind even though I knew that the thought was silly.

I was grumpy for the rest of the day. I strode forward in a rage and nobody had better get in my way! Rylie sensed that it would be an eventful day. He knew just what buttons to push today and he pressed all of them. One thing he didn't know was that on a day like today he shouldn't have taunted me. I stormed through the front doors of the school with a thundercloud hanging over me. I shot death rays at anyone who crossed my path. Randy knew as soon as he saw my face.

"Bad night?"

"Horrible!" I replied past clenched teeth. I almost bit my tongue off trying not to snap at him. I knew he was just being a friend and that I had no reason to be mad at him but right now the rational side of my brain wasn't working. I smiled tightly at him and he got the message.

"Just call on me if you need me." He said, smiled at me and walked into the classroom. I gritted my teeth as Rylie spotted me and walked over me grinning maliciously.

He slammed my locker door shut so I would have to unlock it again. He knew that I hated this, and he smirked at me before walking into the classroom with his two henchmen beside him. He was the biggest guy in our classroom and his posse followed him around like a bunch of obedient lapdogs. I grabbed my books and shoved my elbow into him on my way in the door. He grabbed the back of my shirt and spun me around. I was ready for him. I brought my book up and slammed it into his jaw.

"Oops, sorry didn't see you there!"

One of his henchmen shot a weak punch at me and I ducked. In a story book move he hit the other dimwit in the nose. I hurried over to my desk shaking with silent laughter. The teacher walked in just as the three sat down at their desks, so regretfully they didn't get in trouble, but at least I didn't either. Rylie turned in his seat and glared at me. I glared right back and then smirked as I watched one of his cronies get up to go and get an ice pack. I know it wasn't kind but, seriously, he had it coming. The best part was that it hadn't even been me that had thrown the punch, in fact I hadn't done anything that anyone could accuse me of. I had a clean record so far but if Rylie kept at it he might have a bloody nose and I might have a blemish on my record.

When we went outside for recess I struggled through the deep snow getting angrier with every step. I was sick and tired of this consistent cold weather and snow. I was fed up with the dreams that kept haunting me. I was mad at Rylie for bullying me and not just leaving me alone. I was just plain annoyed at everyone and everything and there was nothing I could do to calm down. I was positively livid by the time I got to the playground and then spun around to march straight back towards the school. A hand grabbed my shoulder and I spun around my hand curled into a fist. Rylie stared at me. He pushed his face into mine and growled at me.

"You had better watch your step around me. You need to learn whose boss around here! Anyone who messes with me learns their lesson pretty fast! Peter, come here! You hold him while Jacob holds his other arm!" Rylie snapped. Jacob and Peter almost fell over themselves trying to do what Rylie asked. Peter was the faster of the two. He lunged forwards to grab my arm. He started dragging me behind a wall. Nobody ever looked there. I was on my own with three big bullies leering at me. It felt stupid, we were just kids, but Rylie had obviously missed that little fact.

Jacob hurried to snatch my other arm. I was too quick for him. I swung my arm out of his grasp. Peter smacked me on the side of the head.

"Stop struggling!" he snapped. I spun around on him and punched him in the nose.

"You!" He growled and attempted to get a better grip on my arm while wiping the blood away from his nose. He went to hit me back but I ducked and head butted him. Rylie simply stood there watching me thrash his supposed buddy. Jacob got around and kicked me. The self - defence I'd learned in Zimbabwe kicked in and I acted purely on instinct. I kicked Peter in the stomach, causing him to loosen his grasp. Then I swung myself away from him and into Jacob. Knocking him over while helping the force to steady myself. With both of his cronies lying on the ground covering their faces Rylie came to life. With a cold glare he stepped over Peter and walked towards me.

"You just made your stupid mistake even worse!" He

spat. "I see you know a bit of defence. Well then let's see how you do against all of us!" Jacob and Peter clambered up again but still hung back a few steps. All three of them came in at me. I hadn't done much group combative, where there's more than one person against you. We had only done a few lessons on how to defend yourself against more than one opponent. You only started learning that stuff seriously in the second level of brown belt.

In karate there is a white belt for beginners. Then orange, red, yellow, and green. After that you have purple, next purple with one white stripe in the middle. Next you start the brown belts. They are the third, second and first 'Kyu'. After that you have black belt. I was only finishing my purple and white belt when we left Africa and I had hoped that by the time I was sixteen I would be on my second 'Kyu'. Then I just had to finish that level and the next to get to black belt. I was still four belts away from black belt and about seven years. Now I would just have to use the little I had learned to defend myself.

Right away I knew that Peter and Jacob had never had a proper defence lesson. Rylie was obviously the main threat here; even so they all had force. Even at nine years old you could see them being teenagers. The way they carried themselves was the way I saw the older kids walking. Rylie, I could tell had some experience. Maybe not a lot, but he had had some. I still thought I could handle them but I might get a few knocks in the process. I watched them coming at me. I could see Rylie getting frustrated as he tried to subtly cue the other two on what to do and where to go. He nodded towards my one side and both of them walked that way. He hissed through his teeth and jerked his head to the other side. Peter walked over to his right and Jacob stayed on his left. Then they advanced. I rushed towards Peter then abruptly switched course and barrelled into Jacob. He groaned and lobbed a punch at me. I caught his fist and twirled it behind his back, wrenching his arm. He yelled. Rylie rushed up behind me but I twisted and kicked him in the knee cap, still holding Jacob's arm. Peter blundered up. I let go of Jacob and swept Peter's feet out from under him. Rylie was up and charging again but he had learned his lesson. I could see that he was more cautious as he turned around me. I drove my elbow into Jacob's back, pushing him away from me. I side stepped around Rylie and swung my arm back, catching Peter. This time Jacob and Peter stayed down.

"You coward!" I yelled at Rylie. "Fight me alone like a real man!" Rylie danced around me. I lunged grabbing his leg and knocking him over. I punched him in the face and then climbed up and calmly walked around the corner.

I waited to be called to the office for getting in a fight. It never happened. Randy said that there was no way that they could tell without getting in trouble. Everyone in the class knew that they were bullies and had seen them bullying me as well as other people. Instead of getting in trouble I got pats on the back. Everyone was glad someone had finally gotten the best of them.

Even though I didn't get in trouble at school Peter's Mom called Dad that evening. She said that Peter wanted to apologize. Afterwards Dad asked me what had happened. I told him everything from the start of the year. He congratulated me on my fine work of beating them senseless. Mom reprimanded him.

"Well, from what I can hear they have been bullying him since he first started at Major Pratt." Dad said. "Would you rather they beat him up?"

"Well of course not!" Mom said, "How can you say that? But he could have talked to the principal!"

"And that would have only made them mad!" Dad explained. "That wouldn't have stopped it!"

"Okay, okay! I was just saying." Mom said and left the subject. Other than that Luke gave me a high five and said that I had showed them how a real man fights.

"They'll leave you alone now! They wouldn't dare challenge you when they know you can beat them to a pulp!"

That was the last I heard of the subject. Other than a few dirty looks the three boys didn't cause any more trouble.

Warm on the outside, cold on the inside

Mom and Dad told us about our summer plans and talked to us about things we could do. They asked us how we were doing in school and kept themselves very much a part of our lives. I guess they were afraid of me slipping back into my depression but it turned out that they should have been more worried about Luke. They knew that he was having trouble because he talked to them about it. I kept all of those things to myself and didn't show anything. Even when my emotions were in absolute turmoil I hid them behind an expressionless face. Maybe that's why I had so much trouble with it but I had always locked my feelings up inside of me and I didn't know how to change now. Luke told Mom and Dad everything and wasn't afraid to show when he was unhappy or even to let us see him crying. He wasn't a cry baby; in fact Dad said he was even stronger because he wasn't afraid to show his feelings. I couldn't let myself just let go and tell Mom and Dad about everything. How homesick I was and how much I wanted to move back to my real home.

I felt mostly frustrated with myself. I felt as if every time I was starting to get better a new struggle came and knocked me over. I felt tired of getting up and trying again, when every time I failed. I just couldn't accept that we were here for good. I had nightmares, that were memories of our home, but surely that was a trick too? I couldn't fathom that our wonderful home could be that bad. So, a few things happened but we had survived! I got scared sometimes but not all the things in my dreams actually happened! We had guard dogs that could kill a guy if they snuck in and we had a twelve foot fence with barbed wire on top. We had guards standing outside our gates to keep us safe, and Dad had a gun. We were safe, we could make it work! I knew that it was unreasonable but I started getting mad at Mom and Dad. I felt as though they had also betrayed me. They had dragged me away from my home and made me think that my home was awful. Every day I got crabbier with them. I snapped at Luke and Katelyn all the time. Anyone would see I walked around looking for a fight.

Like every other phase I went through this too passed. As we neared summer and we saw the first sign of grass, around the edges of our lawn I started getting better again. I could tell Mom and Dad were frustrated with me, but no manner of punishment they had administered had changed my behaviour. I had behaved sullenly, like a, well, like a two year old brat. I felt bad for all the trouble I had caused but I still had to squash down some bad feelings occasionally.

We saw our first robin and watched as the snow receded. Spring was on its way out and summer was pushing its way in. By late June we were getting ready for the end of school. One day I asked Randy how long the summer break was. "Is it two or three weeks?"

"What?" He stared at me.

"Oh." I realised right away that it wasn't the same as in Zimbabwe. "See, in Zimbabwe we normally have six weeks off for the summer, three off in winter and a week in the middle, besides long weekends."

"You poor things!"

"Not really, remember we also got out at one o'clock every day."

"Oh, right." We walked in silence for a while. Randy spoke up again. "Only four more days of school!"

"Yeah, I can't wait! So how long are the holidays?"

"Two months!" He exclaimed happily, "Of absolute freedom!"

"Wow!" I said, smiling.

"Oh yeah!" Randy yelled into the warm air, pumping his fist in the air. I laughed and he turned around. "What are you laughing at?" He asked.

"Humph! Nothing" I said suppressing a snicker.

"You're laughing at me!" Randy said, profaning hurt.

"It's nothing. Really, I mean, it only would have qualified for lunacy!" It wasn't really that bad, but for some reason I couldn't stop laughing. Randy was soon doubled over in laughter too. The busses pulled up and people kept giving us side long glances, obviously thinking we had lost it. Randy and I didn't care, I was on top of the world and nobody's weird glances were going to change that.

The end of school came and summer started. Mostly we had to go in to the office with my parents, but it wasn't that bad. Most of the time Luke and I played outside in the vast expansion of yard.

Mom got two weeks off and Dad got one. We found out about a camping place and bought a tent to go camping. It was quite a long drive but it was worth it! It was beautiful! They had a few cabins at one end of the lake and the campsite was close to the huge lake. There was a nice playground and beach.

We had been getting along a bit better financially and just before we came we bought a little boat. When we drove up I was suddenly whisked to another world. I saw a dirt track leading into the trees and once again I was back home.

Mom was talking to me but I was too engrossed in petting the elephants as they sniffed around us.

We were on a game drive and it was night time. I could hear the lions roaring in the distance but I wasn't worried. They were far away and settling down for the night. Katelyn patted my cheek and I glanced down. She smiled up at me sweetly. We petted the elephants a bit more before we drove on. We weren't going fast and two of the younger elephants ran after us. We all laughed as one of them stuck his trunk inside and sniffed around. The driver stopped and the youngsters pushed their heads down towards us.

Suddenly pain racked my body. I gasped at the force of the razors, raking my chest. I felt like screaming. I blinked and the images faded. The pain receded a little bit but wouldn't let its hold loosen fully. I looked around confused and unsure of my surroundings. I came back down to earth and found myself floating with a life jacket in the water. Once I fully regained my senses the pain ebbed away, until it left me completely.

"Are you okay?" Luke called from the back of the boat.

"Yeah, fine." I replied, still reeling, trying to grasp where I was. Eventually my memory returned and I remembered setting up the tent the day before and how we had gotten ready to go out boating.

"You were leaning too far out to the side and when I stopped you went flying overboard. Man are we lucky you weren't caught by the propeller!" Dad exclaimed as I climbed back aboard.

I was shaking but I wasn't sure if that was because of the shock or the sudden plunge into the cold water. On the beach the water was nice and warm but here it was in the shade. It wouldn't have been so bad if I had been expecting it either. I was in my swimming shorts any way's so it didn't really matter. Mom wrapped me up in a towel and handed me some water to drink. I sipped at it thankfully.

Three days later just before we left we walked down to the beach one last time. Seagulls flew overhead and for one fleeting moment I was calm, but it wasn't a peaceful calm, it was more like the calm before a storm. I looked out over the glassy water and something inside me changed. I folded inwards and the pain almost overcame me, but I managed to straighten up fully and put a mask over my feelings.

We arrived at home late that night. I stormed down to my room and slammed the door. I heard Luke walk into his room and collapse onto his bed with a sigh. I sighed too and put on my pyjamas. I rolled over and let the tears drip onto my pillow, the ache inside me pushed to a new intensity. I heard Dad letting off steam upstairs and felt bad for what I had caused. Our lovely week off had come to a crashing halt about two hours from home. One little mistake, just a few words said wrong and Dad sparked. For the rest of the way home Dad yelled at us, ranted over and over about how lucky we were, or we sat in an awkward silence.

That's the way it always happens though. I reasoned resentfully. *Dad only ever thinks of the bad sides of things, he never sees our side of the story!* I fumed on until eventually my mind slowed and I fell into a fitful sleep.

Mom put us into swimming lessons and I went to the pool three times a week. They tested me to see what level to put me in and I was put into level six. I was the youngest in my group, but I liked my instructor and I moved ahead quickly. I had grown up swimming and we had, had a pool in Africa so I was used to being in the water. Once my swimming instructors saw my potential they suggested that I try out for the swimming team. I got in easily and I discovered a great way to get rid of my anger. In the water I felt free; I could immerse myself in my swimming and forget about the outside world. Underwater it was quiet and peaceful, I loved the way I could glide through the water without a care. I could race against my feelings of frustration and depression, and win.

When we went back to school I felt so disappointed. I felt like there was something that hadn't been fulfilled that I had been counting on to happen. I moped around for the first few weeks and then picked up the routine again and was off. That's the way it normally was, I hated coming back to school after a holiday, but once I fell back into the routine I was okay.

We got the big news two weeks before Thanksgiving. A letter arrived in the mail to tell us that we had been granted our landed immigrancy status. Dad took us out to supper and we were all allowed to miss school the next day. We went into the office but were able to go over to Gary and Lucy's for the day. Mom and Dad came over at lunch time and Lucy made a delicious spread.

It was a day of relief for Mom and Dad especially. Finally we had something tying us here; we had something to help keep us here. Luke was happy too, he felt like finally things were falling into place. He stopped feeling so depressed and things got better for him. Katelyn couldn't understand the importance of what was going on but she did pick up on the festive mood, and she too felt happier. For me nothing changed. I still got mad at everyone around me and everybody's happy mood seemed to bring them closer together. I wasn't feeling happy so this only made me feel more like an outsider, someone who didn't belong. And yet I knew I could change that if I wished, the problem was that I couldn't bring myself to accept that we were here for good now. I couldn't accept that Canada was supposed to be my home, I couldn't and I wouldn't.

For Thanksgiving we went over to Gary and Lucy's for

the day and their parents were there. We had a fun day but the whole time I couldn't help thinking, *a year ago, oh what I wouldn't give to go back to a happier time when none of this was going on.* I knew that the situation in Zimbabwe had been bad, but now that I was out of the circumstance I just couldn't believe that it could really be that bad. How could I miss it so much if it was bad? This line of thought pushed its way into my mind like a worm crawling through an apple. It turned over and over in my mind. Eventually I pushed it out but it left doubt in my mind and that was even harder to dispel.

One song, one important change

Finally one day I had another fight with Luke and Dad lost it. He yelled at me for twenty minutes straight. That night I let the horde of emotions seethe through the careful lock I kept on the cupboard of thoughts that were dangerous for my sanity. Tears ran down my face, and this just added another feeling to the crushing weight already on my shoulders. I felt horrible. How could I be so selfish as to feel self-pity when people were still stuck in Zimbabwe and dying? I felt a self-loathing so deep it cut me worse than the pain, but then the crushing grief washed over me again and I succumbed to it. I gasped quietly and tried to stem the flow of feelings that pushed me down into despair. I heard footsteps coming down the stairs and quickly closed my eyes, hoping to have a peaceful look on my face, instead of bitterness, which would have revealed what was going on inside of me.

Dad came downstairs and stopped for a while as was his routine - listening for any sound. I could hear Luke's steady breathing and saw Dad's dark figure stop in Luke's doorway. He walked in and came out a few minutes later. Then he stopped to make sure I was asleep. I made myself go limp so that when he came to check on me I would appear to be asleep. I shouldn't have worried; Dad turned and walked back up the stairs. A newer resentment churned in me, if this is what he did when he thought I was asleep, I guess that would explain his behaviour in the daylight! I tossed and turned unable to get to sleep. This pattern continued for weeks on end, and I became a grump, making sure everyone knew that they should stay out of my way. I stormed everywhere and glared in every direction. Dark circles appeared under my eyes and wouldn't leave. My long time enemy returned and that only intensified my sleepless nights, I just couldn't seem to shake the nightmares, but then suddenly one day the anger turned inwards. I couldn't say what changed me but something inside of me fell into place. I wouldn't talk to anyone anymore, but I wasn't sad or depressed, I was so angry with myself that I started to get better. I realised that the people I was so mad at were the people trying to help me, they cared about me and I was pushing them away. It was finally a breakthrough for me, I was healing.

Life moved on and when I look back, it was from that point, when I changed my mind set that time began to fly by. I started to feel like I needed to stop and catch my breath, but life doesn't wait for anyone, so I kept up the headlong sprint, trying to stay caught up. It wasn't always a bad thing though, because this made me pleasantly tired so I fell straight to sleep at night, and it didn't give me time to dwell on the past. It was a routine that I needed, just the right thing to keep me going. I began to feel happy, within the surroundings of the present, instead of wishing for the past.

Mom and Dad noticed the change and one day at the supper table I smiled and told them about my day. It was such a small thing, but I had locked myself up inside my head for so long that this made Mom and Dad 'pleased as punch'. They smiled at each other and then at me. That night I went downstairs and hummed tunelessly, just for the sake of humming. Again it was something so small, yet so significant for me. I hadn't hummed or talked about myself without prompting for so long that this was something huge. I had finally found out that I could be happy here in this new country, even if I missed my home country.

We had been looking at songs in language arts now and our teacher had given us one that we had to try and find a message in. I had typed out an interpretation of what the song could mean to me, but it hadn't meant much at the time, now the song made more sense to me and it seemed to hold a key. It seemed to be talking about my life, I suddenly realised. I looked back at my interpretation and found that what I had put down sub-consciously was something that I knew inside of me, but hadn't realised at the time. The words I had typed out were just words at the time, but now they were something from the heart. I went to school early the next day and walked to the computer lab. I drummed my fingers as I waited for the file to load, then I pulled up my interpretation and read through it again.

'I feel that the song is inspired by a hard experience of the person that wrote it. I feel that I can connect with what the song is saying because lately that's how I feel. For me it's encouraging because now I can hope for a brighter light in the future, a rainbow as the song puts it. I guess I need to survive the storm so that I can see the rainbow.'

It was a short answer but the teacher said that it was very advanced for someone my age. I guess that was to be expected because recently I felt like I was a lot older in mind than in body, because of the things I had been through. I fought back the wave of self - pity at that thought, I didn't want to go back to that place again, it would suck me in and wouldn't loosen its hold if I gave in. I looked over the song again, with a new sense of satisfaction; it was like this song was written for me.

Rainbows at the end*

Everything seems to be, going wrong,
Can't be in a room, and get along.
Nobody, understands,
You feel like you're all alone.
Remember, it might be you,
So don't lash out at them, for trying to help you through.
Don't get angry just because you are afraid,
Don't lash out, because of your bad day.
Let yourself out, from the walls in your head,
Sing a song, or go out with a friend.
But always, oh yeah always, look at the light ahead.

Chorus
That when you've got to remember,
There's a rainbow at the end,
That's when you've got to look at,
Your family and your friends.
They are all there, to push you on,
They're all there, to get you where you belong.
They're all trying to help you, don't push them away,
And always look ahead at the brighter day.

When you're tired and you want to stop,
When you feel you just can't keep going,
You're so tired from walking,
And you've forgotten how to run.
It seems you're walking on a treadmill,
It goes faster and faster, and it won't stop.
The rain starts a pounding,
Thunders ringing in your ears,
Lightning flashes and you draw in a ragged breath.

---

* Song is written by Arlene Coleman

Chorus

You emerge from the rain storm, you win the race,
Now hold your head up high.
And then with a victors smile,
You raise your fist to the sky.
Don't you dare forget the friends who,
Pushed you along and got you through.
They helped show the world the real, true, you.
They pushed you up, when they could've torn you down,
They made you smile when you wanted to frown.
They showed you the storm would end,
They are your family and friends.
Chorus
They helped you remember,
There's a rainbow at the end,
They helped you see them,
Your family and your friends.
They were all there pushing you on,
They all helped to get you where you belong.
They all stayed close, so glad you didn't push them away,
They showed you that there would be a brighter day.
They showed you it would be, and now it sure is,
A brighter, clearer, better, day.

I got up and walked to the class room. I was still about
ten minutes early so I took extra care to put everything in
order for the day and get ready for the first class. I kept myself
busy until everybody else arrived, that way I wouldn't have
time to dwell on my earlier thoughts of self-pity, I wouldn't
let myself go down that road again, not now, not today.

Days of bliss dashed into despair

After that demon was conquered nothing exciting happened any more, but that was a huge relief. I felt like I'd had enough excitement for five lifetimes. Winter break came and went and we spent a week at Wellman Lake again, in one of the cabins. We went sledding on the lake and we rented a snowmobile for two days. We had lots of fun and it was amazing just how happy I could be, even when it was freezing cold. If I could just let go and relax I didn't doubt that I would be a lot happier, but something in my being couldn't seem to set free the hold Africa had on me.

When we got back we spent two nights at Gary and Lucy's and then it was time to go back to school. I had Randy over for a sleepover and we grew even closer. He was indeed my best friend. Before I knew it, it was my birthday again and I invited seven boys from my class to come to the birthday party. It turned out that Randy's birthday was the day after mine, so we combined our birthday parties and had them at the same time. We went to the 'Russell Inn' where they had a Pizza Hut and then went swimming at the pool afterwards. We went down the water slide and Randy's Mom - who was a great baker - made us a cake with a dolphin on top with coke balls and icing. It was the best birthday ever and we had lots of fun.

Luke, Katelyn and I started to wish for another pet, preferably a dog; like we had had in Africa, but Mom and Dad told us we couldn't have a large one, because we no longer had the room for a big dog to roam around. Luke and I agreed to help look after a dog and decided that a small dog would be best.

A little while later we found some puppies being sold really cheap so we got one. It was a little toy poodle, and just the right size. The poodle was apricot in color and we named her Trixie. I felt really and truly happy, I almost glowed with contentment. When I looked back on that year it was the first year in Canada that I really enjoyed myself. The year sped by, instead of dragging on. I could hardly remember a lot of the year, because I seemed to be double taking the whole time. This was a good thing because now I could look back on it fondly, instead of resentfully.

Our second summer was a little like our first because we went to Wellman Lake then too, but in so many ways' it was different. I didn't lock everybody else out now, and we were a family once again. The best part for me was that I was now a part of that family, instead of looking on from the outside. I was still on the swim team and I won a few ribbons, it was still my release when I was frustrated and I hadn't lost my love for the water.

Over the summer we also went to visit some friends in Saskatoon, Saskatchewan. Mom and Dad had known them in Zimbabwe, before they had moved to Canada. When things got really bad they tried to help us get into Canada. On the day that we were held at gun point they had called and tried to persuade Dad one last time to consider moving to Canada. Dad said that if they could find him a job here, we would come. Kalvin had then called around until he found out that Gary and Lucy were looking for someone to help them at the plant.

Once again the summer passed but this time I went back to school cheerfully and excited to see all of my friends once again. I quickly got used to the schedule of the grade five classroom. We had a split class with the grade four's this year, but all of the grade fours were split into two classes, so half when with the grade three's and half went with us. I was glad that the grade fives hadn't been split up into two classes, because I was afraid that Randy and I might be split up. I had lots of other friends too, but Randy and I were like bread and butter.

One thing that I had discovered as soon as we had started learning how to read in grade one, was that I loved it. Reading gave me a chance to escape my own world and enjoy traveling to so many different places through the words of authors. I could see and do so much, just by opening up a book. I was a strong reader and I read quickly. This enhanced my spelling and almost all other aspects of my schooling. It helped me in so many ways that it wasn't just a pleasure, but it was also beneficial to my work. I read all the time, finishing two or three thick books a week. There was a section in the library that was restricted for older children. The librarian had decided what was too thick, or too hard a read for our age group and she would separate those books from the others. She came to know me quickly and she didn't hesitate to let me through those boundaries. She knew that I could read really well, with comprehension that surpassed my age, so she would even ask me to recommend books for her sometimes. By the end of my time in that school, we knew each other very well.

Dad got promoted to a higher position, this was nice for all of us, as it included a raise in his salary, but this also meant that he was required to be on call, and work longer hours. He would leave early in the mornings and get home late at night. We saw less and less of him. Even when he was home Dad seemed to be more stressed than normal. Mom and Dad had never been super high strung. They didn't get angry often and not without good cause. We had lots of fun together and in truth, they were our friends in many ways. We were an extremely close family so this enforced distance of Dad, now that he was so busy, was almost hurtful. I knew it was silly because there were so many kids in my class whose parents were divorced or lived separately, or were away from home for long periods of time, but I couldn't help it. I missed sitting down to breakfast with him in the mornings and spending our evenings together. We quickly learned to adjust, and moved on, getting over each obstacle in our path.

Time passed in a blur, it was like I was running but my feet never really touched the ground; never gave me a chance to catch up with what was going on. It was weird though, it sometimes felt as if time was dragging by during the day, but when I looked back on the day when I was going to bed, it seemed to have gone by so fast! I still had to battle the ghosts of my past from dragging me under in their grasp but it got easier with time. I lost the feeling of it being unbearable and it became easier to fight.

One day in November when I came home from school we got some major news. After I found out I jumped up and down for the rest of the day. Dad's parents were coming to visit over the Christmas holidays! All of us were over the moon! Dad and Mom had already booked the two weeks of Christmas break off so that we could be with them and we were going to go with them to Wellman Lake! After that time dragged by even more, but the weird feeling when I looked back over the week and saw it gone, was still there. It confused me because I was so anxious for the Christmas holidays that I was sure time would slow down, but I still had the feeling of time flying by, faster than I could keep up.

Grandma and Grandpa arrived two days before the

Christmas holidays but we weren't doing much in class, so Mom and Dad let Luke and I stay home. We had to pick Granny and Grandpa up at the Winnipeg airport, because Russell didn't have one, but we didn't mind. Even though the drive was really long we stopped along the way and got treats. We got to airport on time and waited anxiously for our Grandparents to appear. I was so excited I couldn't stand still. I was jumping up and down and jabbering on aimlessly, but I couldn't stop. We hadn't seen them in what felt like centuries, but was really just two and a half years.

It felt like we waited hours, but it was just minutes. Finally I caught a glimpse of Grandma and I vaulted over the short wall in front of me that separated the bystanders from the people coming off the plane. I ran up to her and flung my arms around her. Grandpa walked up with the luggage and I hugged him too. By then Mom, Dad, Luke and Katelyn had caught up with me and were all sharing tearful hugs. Tears streamed down Mom and Grandma's face. I hugged them both as we walked out of the airport into the frigid air. A wave of Déjà vu swept over me as we piled their stuff into the car. Could it be two years already? I fought back tears, once again shamed of myself. *Just suck it up!* I repeated over and over again, in my head. *Get over yourself! You cry more than a girl watching a soap opera!* It worked. By the time we had pulled out of the parking lot I had managed to plaster a smile on my face that could pass for joyful. When we arrived home the smile was genuine. Grandma and Grandpa were sleeping downstairs in the guest room. We led them down the stairs and showed them too their room. It was already late when we got home, but we didn't go to sleep for a while. We had a late supper and chatted for a while. Mom had to take Katelyn to bed eventually and still we didn't go to bed. When we did, finally, go to bed - at about three in the morning - my cheeks ached from smiling. I went to bed happy and content. I felt whole, like something that I hadn't even realised was missing, was here now. I felt complete again.

When I woke up around ten the next morning Grandma and Grandpa were still in bed. I snuck into their room and crawled under the sheet. I snuggled up close to my Grandma, and closed my eyes, thankful for the feeling of peace that settled over us. When Luke came into the room a little while later, Grandpa told us stories, like he had when we were with them in Zimbabwe. Then we talked about how we were settling in and how school was going. When we went up for brunch it was twelve thirty. We had a delicious brunch and then we went sledding. We came back laughing late that afternoon. Dad had added to the huge drift by the roof, so that we could sled off of it with Grandpa. We had done it before, but this time was special.

Two weeks later I lay in bed pondering philosophies people had about life. Was it better to have an unbearably sweet candy when afterwards it makes you cry to think of it, or not to have ever tasted the candy at all? If you had something wonderful and it was yanked away from you, was it better to never have had it at all, than to suffer the pain left in its wake? I wasn't sure. Many people said that it was better to have love and then lose it than to never have loved, but right now it sure didn't feel that way. Grandma and Grandpa had left that afternoon and I felt heartbroken. I felt like the hole in my chest was ripped open again. It stayed this way for a while but then I moved on and could talk about that time fondly again. In the end I was glad that I had had that time with them.

When we went back to school Randy and I arranged another sleepover at his house. He had come to my house previously but this was the first time that I was going to his house. We took the bus to his house after school on Friday. We went and put our things in his room; then we went and played outside. His Mom called us in for a snack and I marvelled at this seemingly simple thing. For me it was hard to imagine your Mom waiting for you every day after school, at home! We didn't get home until after six or seven most nights! And then for snack she had made fresh muffins with homemade jam. It was delicious! After our snack we went outside again, still wiping jam off of our faces.

"How does your Mom find the time to come home and make you freshly baked snacks each day?" I asked when we got outside.

"She stays home all day." Randy replied simply. I gaped at him, feeling naive. This idea was new to me. I knew that Mom had stayed home in Zimbabwe, but here everything seemed to be so much faster paced, and busy. I had heard that some of the Moms did manage to stay home, but the thought was foreign to me.

"You mean that your Mom stays home all day, every day?" I asked again, feigning quiet curiosity.

"Yup! She sure does!" Randy said and we slid onto the next topic.

When I got home the next afternoon I was unbelievably happy. I smiled for the rest of the afternoon and we were together as a family for the day because Dad had gotten the day off. We played monopoly and charades and ordered pizza for supper. We hadn't eaten out as a family for ages and this evening was special. We laughed until our sides hurt and our insides felt like jelly. When we went to bed that night I felt like I was floating.

The next week also proved to be a happy one. The outlook was really cheerful, I had been happy for a while but now I was floating and loving every Moment. One day I woke up and found that, to my great surprise, Canada was my home now. I loved it here. I also realised for the first time that my accent was gone. It had disappeared quite a while ago, but this was the first time that I took note of it. I had found a place where I could be content, and it was right here, in Russell, Manitoba, Canada, my home.

Time continued to pass quickly until one day my joyfulness was replaced with fear. Fear that everything was going to shatter, and that I was going to have to move away from my perfect world of happiness. Cold fear that I wouldn't be accepted in my new home, and then fear of leaving everything that was now familiar behind gripped me. Once was enough! I wanted to scream, but I couldn't find the words to say it. I sat in the car and thought bitterly back to the day it first started happening.

Dad called us into their room one Saturday morning. We read the Bible together and then afterwards we lay there on Mom and Dad's bed. Finally Dad spoke up.

"There's something that we want to talk to you kids about."

My first thought was that we were in trouble.

"We're thinking about moving to Alberta." - I almost choked.

"What?" I gasped out.

"Now just calm down." Mom interjected. "We've visited with Kyle and Gina and there's an opening for a computer store there. For reasons you don't need to know about, your Dad and I have given our notice at Pascal's Milling, and we need to find other jobs. If there is an opening here in Russell we will stay, but for now we haven't found a job yet."

Keep looking! I wanted to scream, but I just lay there in a shocked silence.

"And I want you to know that wherever we go, we will be as a family and we will be just fine, we'll all go through it together." Dad added.

Well it turned out that Dad didn't find another job so Mom and Dad decided to start their own business…In Alberta.

So now we were packed up and headed off to Alberta

leaving all of our friends behind us, as we drove out of the town limits. I remembered feeling excited at one point. This was like an adventure, we could meet new people and make new friends and Mom and Dad had promised to come and visit often. It was a twelve hour drive to High River, Alberta from where we had lived. By the time we left, all traces of excitement were gone and a feeling of hopelessness was left in its wake. Mom and Dad had become really stressed ever since we started packing and that really affected the way they acted. Now they snapped at us for the littlest things and I started feeling like I should avoid them, just so that I wouldn't get into trouble for every little thing. When I looked back in the next few years I would realise that this was a turning point, and that nothing was ever going to be the same again.

On August sixth, almost three years after we had first moved to Russell Manitoba, I sat in the back seat of our 'Envoy' on my way to Alberta. Luke, Katelyn and Dad behind us in the U-Haul, one little tear rolled down my cheek, once again a sense of Déjà Vu overwhelmed me and it was all I could do not to go into a full on panic attack. All of my friends and new family were behind me, and I was leaving them behind. Mom turned around at that point and saw that one little tear, making tracks down my cheek.

"What are you crying for?" She snapped and turned her eyes back to the road. That was the very first time that I can remember resenting my Mom. I felt like I had just been slapped across the face, for falling off of my bike. *Why should I get in trouble for feeling sad that my life is being shredded again?* I yelled, but she couldn't read my mind, so she didn't hear a thing. It seemed ironic to me that just when I was perfectly happy here, my world had to be ripped away from me again. I felt like the universe was conspiring against me, trying to make sure that I was never comfortable for more than a few weeks. Every time I just started to settle in something happened that changed my life again. The nightmares had stopped a while ago, but I felt like I was having one now, I just didn't want to accept that I was moving again. I was losing all my friends and everything that had grown familiar to me, again. I felt my world slip through my fingers again as we kept on driving, away from everything that I had grown to love, and away from my home. I was alone again, trapped in the utter despair that came with the memories of the last time I had moved, and how long it had taken me to feel happy again. I fought against the tears and clutched my chest, trying to hold myself together and struggling to cope with the pain that racked through me.

Déjà Vu

We spent the night at a hotel because we had only left Russell after lunch, so we would have had to drive all night to get to Alberta. We went swimming, and for a while I forgot all of my earlier resentment. We ate supper at a nice place across the street from the hotel before turning in for the night. For a while that evening I could imagine that it really would be alright, we were going to make it through this, and we were going to stick together like a family should.

When I woke up the next morning we went down for breakfast together and then set out early again. I dozed along the way, and then watched a movie with Katelyn. It's surprising how entertaining 'Tinkerbelle' could be when you were bored out of your mind. The trip was twelve hours long and we had traveled four hours the day before. We stopped twice along the way to take our dog for a walk and to check on 'Cally cat'. We bought drinks and snacks for along the way. It was fun at first, but after a while it became really annoying. We reached our destination just after four o'clock. We were staying with friends that we had met the first time we came to Alberta. We had been to Alberta to get our landed residency about a year before. A friend had introduced us to Kyle and Gina, and we had ended up staying with them, and as a result had gotten to know them. They were very kind to us when we had been there the previous time and they offered to help us get ourselves set up in Alberta. It was at a time, however, when the oil industry was booming and a lot of people were moving to Alberta. There were no houses for sale, so for now, until we bought a house, we were going to stay with Kyle and Gina.

They met us at the front door and told us where we could park the trailer full of our possessions. They then showed us to our rooms and let us have a few moments to get settled in. We explored the house a little bit and Luke and I discovered a play room. Then we went and sat down in the living room and talked to Kyle and Gina until Mom and Dad came downstairs. Kyle invited us to go outside and explore, so Katelyn, Luke and I headed outside into the warm air. They had a trampoline and a swing set. Katelyn wanted to play in the sandbox for a while then we pushed her on the swing. When we finally came in breathless and hot, Gina had a jug of iced tea waiting for us. It was cool and sweet and soothed my throat on the way down.

We had supper around six - thirty and then we stayed up and played downstairs while Mom and Dad talked to Kyle and Gina. When we went to bed that night I cuddled up with the teddy bear that had come from Africa with me. Even though I was too old for it now it was special to me and I fell asleep quickly. When I woke up it was to bright sunshine and I couldn't help but feel enthused about the move, maybe it wouldn't turn out as bad as I'd first thought it would.

Dad was leaving to go back to Russell for the rest of our furniture and we would see him in three days' time. Gina packed Dad some lunch and snacks for the way, and after we had all kissed him goodbye he drove up the winding hill that was Kyle and Gina's drive way and disappeared, still waving goodbye. After breakfast Luke and I went to play outside while Mom got a bit of business done. Kyle had to get to work, but he had an office in the house, so he worked there most of the time. When Kyle had to go out and check on things in the workshop we went with him and looked around. After that things got boring for the next few days.

Dad drove into the yard with all of our furniture, right on schedule, Friday afternoon. He was very tired so on Saturday we had a lazy kind of day and Dad caught up on some sleep. On Sunday we went to a meeting and on Monday Mom and Dad had to start working. They started looking for a space in which to start the business as well as a house. At this point in time the oil business was booming and everyone was moving to Alberta. Things were going crazy and a lot of people were looking for homes, the only problem was that none were for sale. As soon as one house opened up there were twenty people all waiting to buy it, no matter what the price or size, because everyone was really anxious just to get a house.

Luke, Katelyn and I all stayed home with Gina and Kyle most of the time but then they went away for two weeks and Mom called in a babysitter. The baby sitter didn't really do anything except play with us and make us food, which was just fine with us. She didn't try to organize our day or tell us what to do; she just stopped us before we did anything bad. The last three weeks of summer were a lot of fun and we did a whole bunch of nothing. One Saturday Gina and Kyle took us to the Calgary zoo and that was really cool, another we went into Calgary with Mom and just had a shopping day. But all good things must come to a close and eventually time and reality caught up with us. It wasn't long before we had to go school shopping and figure out what school we were going to be registered in. As more houses were coming up for sale in Nanton it seemed that it was most likely we were going to live there, so Mom and Dad registered us at the school in Nanton.

The last Saturday before school started Mom and Dad

took us with them when they went house shopping. It was a simple little blue house with an unfinished basement, but even when we had booked an appointment there were two cars driving past outside, waiting for us to be finished so that they could look at the house. It was a nice house, though it was small and it had a little porch in the back. It had one bathroom with a little shower adjoining to the master bedroom and one just down the hall. It only had two rooms but we would manage and the room that was across from the master bedroom, Katelyn could stay in so that she'd be close to Mom and Dad. Luke and I could sleep downstairs and hopefully we could get the basement finished soon. The price was good and we went out for dinner to finish the deal.

We couldn't move in for a few weeks but it was a huge relief for Mom and Dad knowing that we did have a house to our name now. Mom and Dad could concentrate on finding a space for their business and then starting it up. They warned Luke and me that we would have to help out a lot and that things would be stressed. That little voice of bitterness crept up in my mind again and it was all I could do not to snap back sarcastically.

"You're going to have to help out a bit more around the house."

Yeah because that would be a change! Are you kidding me? As if we haven't been under a lot of stress ever since we moved to Canada. At age eight I was basically told to grow up and start helping out. Yeah, it's been a great childhood when I never even had a chance to live it! Oh, but now you're feeling the stress and everything is suddenly our fault!

I tried to squash that annoying voice, because even though I was mad at the moment, deep down I knew that it wasn't true. Mom and Dad had tried to do what was best for us. And I had had a chance to live like a kid. Mom and

Dad had always tried their very best for us and at the least we could try to help out as they made sacrifices for us.

When the first day of school arrived I was trying to convince myself that it wouldn't be all bad.

It won't be that bad, it'll be okay. I tried to convince myself, but another voice piped up - *You're kidding it'll be a disaster!*

I argued with myself, trying to squish the other voice that told me it wouldn't go well, and then with a deep breath, I walked into the school. My breath and courage all whooshed out of me as I took in the massive blob of kids that all turned to stare at me, or so I imagined. Mom offered to walk Luke and I to our classrooms but with hurried goodbyes we turned her offer down and waded into the sea of bodies towards our doom.

Since when are you so melodramatic? Come on, this is just like when you started in Manitoba. Give it a rest!

I sucked in another deep breath and opened the door to the grade six classroom. I walked over to the nearest empty desk and sat down. I put my backpack on my desk and lay my head down on it like a pillow. I sighed and wished that I could be back with my friends, starting a new year in Manitoba. This was supposedly a big year; this would be the first year we could go on school teams and truly be in junior high. I sighed again and looked around me. There were groups of kids talking animatedly all around me, they were all friends, I thought, they already knew each other. I didn't know anyone. A wave of loneliness I hadn't felt in ages stole over me. I felt like I was going to be sick. It felt like hours before the bell rang and the teacher walked into the room. I couldn't remember his name, so I just listened to what the other kids called him, I quickly found out that his name was Mr. Daserly, but he said we could call him Mr.D. After 'O Canada' he asked all of the new kids stand up and tell everybody a little bit about themselves. Unfortunately I was the only new kid. I stood up and felt like I would fall over, my legs were so shaky. Mr. D asked me to walk up to the front of the classroom. I walked up and just stood there.

"Why don't you tell us your name?" Mr. D asked.

"Ummm…" I started, trying to remember how to speak. "My name is Thomas." I said and then just stood there.

"Where are you from?" Mr.D prompted.

"I'm from Zimbabwe, Africa." I said miserably. "I moved to Canada three years ago. I lived in Russell Manitoba for a while and then we moved here at the start of August."

"That's interesting." Mr.D continued, unphased by my lack of enthusiasm. "Why don't you show us where Zimbabwe is on the map? I don't think many of us have heard of that."

So I walked over to the map hanging on the backboard along the side of the classroom. I circled Zimbabwe with a whiteboard marker. The class asked me a few questions about where I was from and then they all told me their names and something interesting about themselves. I quickly realised that the main things that formed friend groups around here were parent's relations, rodeo and hockey. I felt a knot forming in my stomach and wished that I'd eaten breakfast that morning.

We got assigned seats and then our teacher gave us an overview of how things would go this year - the usual things that go on the first day of school. After the first recess there was an assembly and after that we got started in organizing our things for classes. Soon it was time for lunch, but when the bell rang the other kids didn't get their lunches out, they went outside first. I found it confusing and it made me feel really stupid, like I had the first day of school in Manitoba. I felt again like this had to be a bad dream and had the silly notion to pinch myself, hoping I would wake up in my own bed at home. I had gone through losing my home once, I didn't want to lose it again, but if this wasn't a dream I guess it was too late.

I hadn't felt this engulfed by loneliness in ages. I walked around the playground to a small corner behind some trees and sunk down, thinking of home. Now I didn't think of Zimbabwe, my home was the little town of Russell, Manitoba. I felt like crying, but that was the worst thing I could do, if someone saw me I'd be stuck with a cry baby reputation forever! The bell rang to go inside and I walked slowly along, sulking just a little bit. I stopped just before the door and took a few deep breaths to try and pull myself together; I'd been doing that a lot today.

The rest of the day got a little bit better. I made two, 'sort of' friends and they sat with me for lunch. When I got home that afternoon and Mom asked how my day had gone I opened my mouth to tell her that it was awful, but then I looked at her and realised just how tired she looked and smiled.

"It was great! I made some friends and I'm really looking forward to it!" I said instead.

"That's great honey, can you look after your sister, she had her first day of kindergarten today!" Mom and Dad had put Katelyn in a High River school because that's where the business would be and they wanted her closer to them.

I took Katelyn from Mom and went to play with her and Luke downstairs. Luke was quiet and seemed a bit moody; we had always gotten along pretty well and had never fought much so I asked him what was wrong. To my great surprise he snapped at me and stomped off to our room. Katelyn fell over and started to cry. I hushed her, knowing that if Mom heard we'd all be in big trouble.

"Shh, shh, honey, it's okay, shh."

Mom was looking a little over the edge today and I really didn't want her coming downstairs to see what was wrong. I wasn't sure whether Katelyn had just had a rough time today or if she was just picking up on all the tension around her, but she seemed to cry a lot that afternoon. I realised that she was just crying a lot lately, forget just this afternoon. I knew that even though she was small and couldn't really understand why all of us were so stressed out, she knew that something wasn't right. She eventually stopped crying and I laid her down for a nap. She didn't want to take one, but I read her a story until she fell asleep on Mom and Dad's bed. I knew that it probably wasn't a good idea, because then she wouldn't sleep that night, but I just couldn't find the energy to look after her right now. I wanted to go and lie down in Luke and my room, but didn't want to face him right now either. I stopped at the door but then went outside instead. It was nice outside and I walked down to the play area. I sat down on one of the benches and sighed. I really wished that our family could just settle down and be happy again, like it used to be.

It's just that right now things are kind of hectic. Once the business gets going and we move into our own house, things will be better. I assured myself and then went back inside feeling a bit better.

A torn family

The next day school didn't go very well. It looked like I was off to a bad start. At lunch break I went to the corner of the schoolyard again and sat down. I felt like crying, but once again I scoffed at myself and told myself to suck it up. For the next few weeks things got a little bit better. I settled in at school a bit more and we moved into our house. Things got worse at home though. Luke and I started fighting about every little thing, both of us convinced that we were in the right and that the other was the wrong one. I missed the friend that Luke used to be to me, but again I quieted the warning bells that rang in my mind and managed to tell myself that things would get better. And things did for a little while, but then they got worse. I started getting made fun off at school and I started lying, just making up random stories. I wasn't sure what made me do it, but I guess I just wanted to fit in. It became harder and harder to get along with everyone at home. I seemed to get in more and more trouble with Mom and Dad and Luke and I fought even more, rather than less. Even Katelyn kept getting on my nerves and I would snap at her. Every night I found it harder and harder not to just sink into the waters of depression again. I hadn't felt this bad in over a year and I couldn't seem to fight it any more.

One afternoon when I was unpacking the dishwasher I

forgot where the pots went. Mom was working in the kitchen getting supper ready so I asked her. She grabbed the pot and wheeled around.

"We've been living in this house for over two weeks now; you should know where they go!" She screamed at me.

I shrank back against the cupboards. She raised the pot above her head and I thought she was going to hit me with it.

"Why do I have to do everything myself?" She yelled, "Can't you do anything right?" I fought back tears as I ran from the kitchen down the stairs and threw myself on my bed. I sobbed into my pillow, all the while cursing myself. I cried until no more tears would come and then exhausted I fell into a fitful sleep. I had my first nightmare in this new, frightening place and I woke up in the middle of the night, drenched with sweat and battling my blankets. I untangled myself from my blankets and snuck up the stairs to the washroom. I splashed cold water on my face and washed the grit from my eyes. I was hungry now, since I hadn't had supper the night before. I walked into the kitchen and looked at the time on the stove. It was three - thirty in the morning and now I was wide awake. I had a headache from my earlier crying fit so I walked back to the bathroom and got some Tylenol. After that I got a drink of water and thought about getting myself something to eat, but the thought of Mom or Dad waking up and getting mad at me again persuaded me to head back downstairs. I slid back into bed and closed my eyes, hoping sleep would find me. Of course it didn't but I had to try. I sat up in bed my shoulders slumped. Despite my early night I was exhausted. I rolled my shoulders and yawned. I turned my iPod on and turned it down low so that it wouldn't wake anyone up. I eventually dozed off around four - thirty, but it felt like absolutely no time had passed before my alarm clock was ringing telling me it was time to get up for school.

I sighed and against better judgement I pressed the snooze button. I rolled over and quickly fell asleep again.

I woke up later with Luke shaking me and saying, "It's eight o'clock!" I jumped out of bed all weariness forgotten. All I needed now was a grand entrance that would give everyone another excuse to make fun of me. By some miracle we made it to school on time and I slid into my seat with no one noticing me.

I couldn't help but wish that this was just a nightmare; I missed all my friends from Manitoba terribly and wished once more that I could just pinch myself and wake up in my own bed in my real home. I finally managed to pick up a routine. Get up in the mornings, get to school, and try to stay inconspicuous. Then when I got home, I squashed down all the sharp comebacks I had to getting yelled at for something that wasn't my fault, sealed my lips together so I didn't get yelled at some more for saying what I really thought until I could finally escape to my room and squeeze my eyes shut so I didn't cry. Lastly I had to constantly suppress all rude thoughts about my family.

At certain times I felt bad about everything I had to say (or think) about my family; because there were times that we were a family again, just like we used to be. The only thing is that we couldn't go one whole day where that happened and we didn't ruin it by going back to our new stressed out, crabby selves. I was frustrated with my family, but mostly with myself. I had heard the saying 'it takes two to tango', or 'it takes two to fight' many times, but that didn't keep me from feeling resentful and thinking that it was all someone else's fault. Every day I struggled to overcome my temper and it seemed that every day I lost. I just couldn't seem to get it under control. At school things got worse. Every night I would lie in bed and feel anger and hopelessness wash through me. I couldn't seem to move forward. I knew that Mom and Dad were trying their very best for us and that part of the reason we had moved was to try and give us a better life, but the stress of starting a new business, financial issues and then all of us kids on top of that was sometimes too much for them. They would get home, angry from something that had gone wrong at the office that day and it just went downhill from there. I couldn't decide what I wanted. Because Dad was getting things started at the new business he worked really long hours and I felt like I hardly ever saw him, but at the same time when I did get to see him I just got mad at him and he got mad at me. I felt resentful because he was never there, but I also felt resentful whenever he was there.

We went along for quite some time like this and I began to wonder if this was what it was going to be like for the rest of my life at home. It was like every day just kept repeating itself over and over. Nothing got better, and nothing really changed. I was depressed but I felt like I couldn't talk to anyone about it. Mom and Dad were obviously too busy to hear about some stupid problems I was having at school and Luke - who I used to talk to about every problem I had - was distant. We were getting older and developing new ideas so we didn't get along as well as we used to; he would easily get mad at me. I felt utterly alone and it felt like there was nothing I could do. One day I wondered if maybe it wouldn't be better if I was alone, physically too, at least then I wouldn't get yelled at all the time and picked on at school.

Every time I would get in trouble I had to swallow back some retort, because I had a lot of them. I didn't tell anyone anything personal, about the troubles at school or how I was feeling, but I wasn't able to tell if that was because of the way everyone was acting, or just because I had never been someone to tell everyone how I felt. Life went on, but it didn't feel like I was getting anywhere.

I missed Manitoba terribly and I got depressed again, but this time I didn't show it as much. When Christmas finally came around the holidays were actually okay, but I dreaded going back to school. The night before we were supposed to go back to school I felt like crying. I was desperate to avoid going back to school, but I couldn't find a way out of it, so the next day we headed off to school and it lived up to my expectations. I couldn't help but feel miserable and the whole day went from bad to worse. I ran away from school twice at the break, but I could never think of facing the fury that would await me at home, if Mom and Dad found out, so I always turned around and walked back to school. This didn't help matters with the other students, but sometimes I just felt like I couldn't take it anymore and I had to leave before I lost it completely.

I walked home with Luke after school in a terrible mood. It was warm for this time of year and a west wind was blowing, so we could expect a Chinook to increase the temperature for the next week or so. Surprisingly Luke and I didn't fight all the way home, and for a little while things seemed to get better. I was cautious as I walked into the house, sure that the day would continue its downward path, but when I walked into the house Mom was smiling down at me and holding Katelyn on her hip. I looked up at her questioningly while I pulled off my snow boots.

"We're going out for dinner tonight." Mom said, a little too cheerfully.

Luke and I exchanged looks with each other and then continued to shed our winter layers.

"And then afterwards we're going to go for a drive." Mom continued, unperturbed by our confused attitudes.

Dad arrived home earlier than usual that night and as things had been really busy at work lately I was surprised he had even made it home for supper, but true to Mom's word we headed out to a Chinese restaurant. It was a very quiet ride to the restaurant but when we got there Mom and Dad seemed in a good mood. I was confused on how things could change so quickly, everyone had been grumpy this morning, but when we all sat down to eat things continued to go smoothly. For the first time in a long time I felt myself relax a bit and I even managed a few genuine smiles. It was eerily like a few evenings that'd we'd had in Manitoba and I had a strange feeling as if I was swallowing pain killers. I knew that the pain would return, but for now I was in my happy world and I didn't want to look at the real world, for fear of what I would see. Even if it was only for a while it was exactly what I needed, after such a long time of feeling like I was shoved into a dark corner. It felt like the warmest sun was suddenly coming out of the clouds.

That night when I lay in bed, I smiled as I thought of the day, rather than fighting back resentment and tears of frustration. I didn't have any bad dreams that night and I got my first good night of sleep in ages.

A new summer, a new house, a new school

After that things got better. Things were still really stressed at home but I could deal with it better. I realised that things weren't the best at school, but it wasn't as bad as I had thought it to be. I did have a few friends and the others kids' teasing was a lot of my fault. I still didn't particularly like it there, but I came to the point where I could see that the biggest attitude problem was me. It didn't make things easier to change my attitude, because I still had a really bad temper, but it helped me to appreciate the attitude of others more and see that it wasn't all their fault.

I still didn't want to go to that school though, so when the end of the year finally arrived I was very happy. I was also a bit worried because I wasn't sure how to broach the subject of switching schools with Mom and Dad.

July passed without incident, we spent our time at the office, but it was actually fine. There was a park a few blocks down from the office where you could go camping and it had a park for Katelyn to play in and a path that ran by the river, at the edge of the park. The river continued out of the park and curved down right behind the office, we found a nice little sandy beach there and we spent a great deal of time there.

One Saturday Dad finally took the day off and left the secretary running the office. Someone had told us that we should try tubing down the river, so we got together one big inflatable boat for Mom, Dad and Katelyn and two tubes for Luke and I.

We went to a corner where there was a place to pull over on the side of the road. We left the one car there and the other at the end of the route we were taking down the river. We slathered on sunscreen and headed off down the river. There were some places where branches hung out over the river and other places where the river was really shallow and someone had to get off their floating device and push the boat. All of us had to wear life jackets and in one deep spot I fell behind the others. I hopped off the tube and started to kick, hoping to catch up again. As I neared them I tried to get on the tube again, but it flipped out from under me, across to the other side of the river. The river was flowing fast in this spot and there was a branch hanging over the river, just ahead. I was dunked under the water and instinctively I grabbed the branch to try and save myself from being bashed against the edge. I tried to pull myself up but the current was too strong. I fought against the current but to no avail, I couldn't get myself up. I managed to bring my head up and heard Mom yelling for me to let go of the branch, but then I got swept under the water again. I tried to bring my head up and bashed it against the branch, hard. I coughed into the water and tried to take a breath but got a mouthful of water. I saw stars and realised I was drowning.

This is it. I thought, *I'm dying, I'm going to drown.*

I relaxed my grip on the branch and giving up all hope I let go of the branch. It turned out that despite thinking this action would kill me, it actually saved me. I bobbed to the surface and gasped for breath. I swam towards the opposite shore and lay there hacking. The others paddled to the shore and picked their way through the brush to my side.

"Great, the tube is wrecked!" Dad yelled.

"I was drowning!" I coughed out.

"No you weren't, nonsense." Dad said, his back to me, still inspecting the tube. Mom helped me up and rubbed my back.

"If you weren't laying back and falling behind us, you would have been fine!" Dad continued, "You have to paddle!"

I was trying! I yelled in my head, all my old resentments welling up inside me.

The rest of the day didn't go very well, my family enjoyed the ride, but the day was ruined for me. I had almost drowned, and all my Dad could do was yell at me. It made me almost wish that I had drowned, I wondered what he would do then. I glared around me and things seemed to go downhill again after that. Luke and I got along a bit better again, but every time I made a mistake, and got in trouble I couldn't suppress the voices inside my head that yelled at the injustice.

In August things started to change. I had liked horses for quite a while and Mom had enrolled me in lessons. I learnt western and started off slow, but I had a lot of fun. After I learnt the basics we started working on loping, and then tricks, different commands, and lead changes. I loved it! It was a place for me to escape from all of my problems, just like reading. I loved how the horses listened to you and it always cheered me up to be around them. Then it became my dream to own one.

In August Mom spotted an ad for an acreage. We drove out here to look at it on the open night and I loved it. It was an old house but had a huge yard. It had a tree house and an open field, a huge garden and the master bedroom was as big as our whole house in Nanton. The master bedroom had a little adjoined room that would be Katelyn's and a big open area, around a fire place. It was a wonderful place that I loved immediately. Mom and Dad seemed to like it too and they made an offer on it. There were a lot of people interested though and when Mom and Dad heard the offer from someone else for the house, they didn't seem too hopeful. I felt let down, but crossed my fingers hoping that we would be the lucky ones to move into that cool place.

Well my wish came true, we worked out a deal over the summer and were to move in a few days after the school year started.

It turned out that Mom and Dad had seen that we weren't happy in Nanton so they asked us if we wanted to move into Cayley School. Luke would be going to high school now, so he was asked if he wanted to go to Nanton or High River. He chose High River and I only had one year left in elementary/junior school. I desperately didn't want to go to Nanton again, so I went to Cayley School. We went to go and look around the school in the last two weeks of summer holidays. It was a small school, with only one hallway, but I said that I would like to go there in the fall.

When the fall came around we all started school, Luke started two days after me and boasted about it freely, teasing me.

"Only one more year and then I'm there too." I reminded him; he just smiled and walked away.

Mom dropped me off at school for the first week, but after that I caught the bus to school and Mom would just drop off Luke and Katelyn. On the first day Mom kissed my cheek outside the school and with one final wave I walked through the doors to my new school - again. I closed my eyes and fervently hoped that this wasn't history repeating itself and hoped that I would be happier here.

I still missed Manitoba and my friends there, but when

I called Randy he seemed more and more distant. Eventually Mom told me to ask him to call me instead of me always calling him. I did and gave him our new number, but I never heard from him after that, and once I started going to school in Cayley it didn't seem as devastating anymore. I made new friends and though I didn't forget about my old friends, I moved on.

The first day was as bad as the rest of them, I nervously walked up to the front of the room and told them where I was from, but after that first introduction, things definitely got better. There weren't many kids in the class, but they were all good friends and they welcomed into their circle with open arms. When Mom picked me up from school that day my smile was genuine and I didn't have to fake it, my relief was huge at being accepted so readily.

We started into the school year and Luke was busy, I had to pick up a few of his chores, because he had to study and had lots of homework. Our lives were hectic, but we got along better as a family again. I still got resentful and angry inside a lot, but I struggled to remind myself that my family had put up with me when I was in bad spots so many times, that the least I could do was to give them a break and to remember that I wasn't always right, and sometimes they did have a point. We all had to do what we had to do, and we all did it to get along. I must admit that in the later months and even the next year or so, I could see again how mean I was. At one point I detested myself and yet I couldn't seem to snap out of my silent fuming. It didn't go unnoticed though; everyone around me could see it and I felt bad. I felt as though life was so unfair and eventually one day Dad sat me down and had a stern talk with me. I felt my resentment flare and I opened my mouth to tell him my side of the story. A small voice inside my head stopped me and I snapped my mouth shut again.

Just listen, He's a lot older than you and knows a lot more.

I'm not sure if anyone else felt the difference in me afterwards but I sure hoped they did. It was still a struggle, but at least I was trying now.

At school things only got better too. School had never been a struggle for me and it still wasn't now, but it meant something. I didn't just do the work because I had to; I put myself into my work, but enjoyed myself outside of class too. I made some really good friends and though things are never perfect, I was so much happier in Cayley than I had ever been in Nanton.

I didn't bear a grudge towards anyone in Nanton; I retained the insight that it had been me, and not so much the others in Nanton. I had made myself miserable, and I had behaved atrociously. I had embarrassed myself there and I just hoped that no one would bear ill-will to me later on. I had not left a good impression.

And as I said before, things were never perfect, but when in life were things perfect? I believed that they were as good as they could get, and I was happy.

A family once again

It got colder outside and snow fell, we didn't get a Chinook for a long time and the snow stayed. Over Christmas we went back to visit Manitoba. We spent a week with Andrew and Alice, some very good friends from Zimbabwe and then went back to spend another week in Russell with Gary and Lucy and our other friends. It was lovely to see them all again and it brought back so many good memories, but I also realised that Manitoba wasn't home anymore, Alberta was. It came with a great sense of relief that I didn't have to drag along this feeling of wanting to go home, because I was home now, I was with my friends and family and they were in Alberta, I finally had a home, where I could stay, my home was where my house was.

At school I quickly developed favourite classes and much to the disbelief of all my new friends Math and L.A. were my favourites. One Monday we received a new assignment that I found to have a knack for. I had already tried my hand at poetry and found that I enjoyed it. I always felt like looking over my shoulder to see who would think it was too girlish for a boy to be doing poetry, but I found that my skill was actually admired. We were only asked to write one poem, but once I started I couldn't stop. I ended up writing seven and I was asked to help others, as I had finished early.

We had a parent/teacher night just a few days after I had

finished my last poem and my teacher told them how well I was doing. When we got home that night Mom asked me why I hadn't told them, or read any of my poems to them. I promptly ran downstairs, plugged in my USB stick and printed off my poems. I ran upstairs and started to read. I tried to ignore the snickers I was sure would erupt, when Dad and Luke heard my poems, but they all sat silently and listened all the way from my first poem to my last.

"Winter

Now the world is covered with snow,
Everyone's inside, with no place to go.
As the pond is slowly covered with ice,
Nothing but a fireplace will suffice.
Winter attacks with a cold cruel bite,
He's always there looking for a fight.
The wind outside gives a mighty howl,
Winters breath is oh so foul.
As the wind whispers down our necks,
On unclothed skin the frost there pecks.
Way down there at the North Pole
Santa works towards his goal.
On Christmas morn we awake to toys,
But only coal for the bad girls and boys.
Snowflake by snowflake builds layer by layer,
No one can escape it not even the mayor!
Snow can be fun but ice is your foe,
It can be dangerous as everyone should know!
In your driveway you're very very stuck,
So pull out your hockey sticks, skates and puck!
I suppose winter can be sweet.
And maybe, just maybe, a little bit neat.
As long as you have a favourite winter sport,
And know how to build a strong snow fort!"

I took a quick look at my family all sitting silently, with open awe at my new found talent; I smiled quickly and then continued.

"Wandering Alone

A small boy cast out on the street,
Left all alone only a beggars scraps to eat,
He gets up and starts his journey,
Wandering alone,
Wandering alone.

A teenage boy walking in the countryside,
He's filthy and tired but no one offers him a ride,
So he continues his journey on,
Wandering alone,
Wandering alone.

An old man lost and cold in the wood,
No one misses him though many should,
So he stumbles along,
Wandering alone,
Wandering alone.

The wolves descend and attack,
Then his struggle ends, his mouth goes slack,
His life's over but...
He believes he's still wandering alone,
Wandering alone,
He thinks forever, wandering alone.

But no...
In his life he helped out many, now
he stands within the gates,
He waits in line with the others waiting for his fate,
He no longer has to wander alone,
He's now joined his family at last, once more, home."

This time I didn't stop, I just kept going.

"Morning Air

The sun bursts forth and chases away the clouds,
Then the beautiful sky is filled with sounds.
During the night, rain has fallen,
Giving the world a new calling.
The sky is lit up like a dancing fire,
Of this amazing scene I could never tire.
The distant horrors of the night,
Oh my, they left us shivering with fright,
But the alarming terrors are now long gone,
While the morning air swells with a beautiful song.
Now in the day we can dance,
We can play and we can prance.
We don't have a care, or a fear,
Because we know that night is nowhere near."

Without a pause I started on to the next poem

"Friends

When your very world is shaking,
And your heart is breaking,
What do you do?
Where do you go?
Who helps you?

If your worst nightmare took place,
If a fierce battle you had to face,
What would you do?
Where would you go?
Who would help you?

You need someone to show the way,
Who'll stay by your side every day?
How will you find them?
Where will you find them?
Who could it be?

Have you ever found your true friend?
Someone who'd stick by you 'til the end,
How did it happen?
Where did you find them?
Who is it?

A true friend is a royal treasure,
They'll always bring you lots of pleasure,
Can you find them?
Where will you look?
Who might it be?"

I took a deep breath before continuing, my next poem reflected more upon my life than personal inspiration and I hoped my family would like this one as well.

"Have Faith, Believe

I stare out the window into the black,
My whole life beside me in a sack.
I'm on my way to another life,
Hopefully one without as much strife.
In this new world I feel all alone,
I'm not quite sure where to call home.
Things are not always what they seem,
But I know life is best conquered as a team.
There's no way you can count on earthly pleasures,
Because true friends are more worthy treasures,

Even across countries, they're still in your heart,
Standing with each other is a friend's part.
I know now their thoughts are with me,
As I travel on, stiff and fearfully
I'm afraid because I don't know,
What waits for me in the country below?
I hope it will be better than my home before
Then with a sigh I walk out of the door.
Now I'm here in this new place,
I try not to hope just in case.
I don't want to be disappointed once again,
I don't know if I could stay sane.
Now I'm here in Canada,
I made the trip from Africa,
I'm sure that here I will be just fine,
The people here are really kind.
So draw strength from my words,
And take flight as the birds.
Though at times it might seem scary,
On the doorstep don't you tarry.
I decided to take a leap
Off I went into the deep,
Then up I came and started to float
I didn't need a life jacket or a boat,
Remember your friends,
And they'll help tie up loose ends."

This last one also meant a lot to me and it was my most recent poem, inspired by the need I felt to show others what this country meant to me.

"The feeling of Freedom

The grass is flowing, my hair is blowing
The wind is humming a melody,
The whole world singing out the joy I feel in me,
The world at my fingertips, freedom
whistling through the air
I know and feel I'm truly free

The cost of freedom is like no other,
Hand in hand sacrifice is freedoms brother.
Reassured in the sacrifice of lives before us,
Such selflessness not even making a fuss,
The courage shines forth in them and we are so grateful
It's because of them that we can know it,
Because of them that we can feel it,
We see it, we are truly free.

When we look all around us we know we have it good
This country's given us all that a country could,
You don't have to sleep with a gun by your bed,
You don't walk around with a knife hanging over your head,
We all know it, we can all feel,
Our whole nation rising to sing it
We are all truly free."

I smiled and looked at my family. They all stared at me
for a second before the applause started. I laughed a little
self-consciously and Mom enveloped me in a huge hug.
"That was magnificent." She told me.
I think I smiled the whole night, even in my sleep.

Home once more

In February Mom and Dad applied for our citizenship and we received the date for when the test was to be taken. We had known that they had to take a test to guarantee that they could get their citizenship, but it was a very big deal at the same time. I was anxious for summer to come and became impatient for the warmth to come. Mom and Dad started talking about all the air miles they had saved up, and as soon as we had our citizenship we would apply for our passports, hopefully by December we might be able to visit South Africa over Christmas holidays. This news made us all euphoric, and in general we were a happy family again.

Mom and Dad took the citizenship test at the beginning of June and a few weeks later we got the results back.

"We passed!" Mom yelled as she flipped through the results.

We all jumped up and down and went out for supper that night. Even though Mom and Dad had been pretty confident they had passed this was a big weight off of their backs. We were going to be Canadian citizens soon!

The ceremony was to take place on Canada day; it was barely two weeks away. We called all of our friends and Family all over the world and all over Canada. Gary and Lucy arranged to fly down for the day of our ceremony and it meant the world to us. As the day drew near and the end of school was just days away we became more and more on edge. Mom took us all out and we bought fancy red shirts for us guys and beautiful red dresses for the two ladies.

On the morning of the big day we got up early and got all of our things together. Mom made sure she had her camera and purse, then we all piled into the truck for the ride to the Calgary airport. On the way there the excitement was tangible in the air and we all bounced in our seats. Mom and Dad seemed as excited as we were and did nothing to stop us from goofing around in the back.

We arrived at the airport and half ran to the elevator and then through the doors into the warm air of the airport. We hurried through the massive hallways of the airport, peering around hoping to get a glimpse of Gary and Lucy. They finally emerged from the throng of people getting off the plane and we all ran towards each other smothering each other in big hugs. Gary ruffled our hair and commented on how big we'd gotten Lucy also remarked on our new height and hugged us fiercely. We walked out of the airport and into the frigid air. Okay, so it wasn't frigid today, it was warm and for us full of promise, but with Gary and Lucy walking beside us pulling a small suitcase for the day brought back strong memories, but today I didn't feel alone, I knew that today I was going to become a Canadian citizen and our friends and family would all be with us, in thoughts if not in body. I must have looked like a complete idiot with a huge grin so big it made my cheeks ache.

We went out for breakfast with them, before making our way through the city of Calgary, to the Prince Edward Park, where the ceremony would take place. All around us were people all dressed in red and white, with maple leaves pinned to their tops. I walked with my family and felt over the moon, this was our day, we were so close now. Waiting for us was our own fan club, we had so many friends there to support us and I couldn't have been happier.

When it was time for us to go and sit down the five of us had to go and sit up front, while our little section of friends had to sit separately. We walked up to our seats and put on the pins they had given us, then the ceremony started. Everyone was reverently quiet and in the background one last bird chirped then all was silent as the ceremony started. It might not have been that dramatic, but I was in my own world, so I wouldn't have been able to tell.

A few guest speakers spoke first and then we were all asked to stand up and repeat the oaths. We all stood and put up our right hands. The lady leading the ceremony said the words first in English then in French and we solemnly repeated the words after her, pledging our allegiance to Canada and to the queen of England. When we were done they slowly called us up to receive our citizenship. We received our legal pieces of laminated paper and shook hands with all the representatives. After the hordes of pictures our little group gathered underneath the flags of Canada. Standing there with all of our friends and family around us I knew that they were the ones that had gotten us here, that had gotten us this far and they would help us get through whatever struggles were still to come. We were Canadian citizens now and though we didn't have any blood family here, the ties that we had with the people around us, were just as strong as blood could have made us. I thought back to the past five years and though it hadn't been easy - and I doubted the next few years would be either - I knew that Canada was my home now and I wouldn't want it any other way. This was our home, this was our family, and we were Canadian.